The SAPPHIRE Affair

ALSO BY LAUREN BLAKELY

The Caught Up in Love Series

(Each book in this series follows a different couple, so each book can
be read separately or enjoyed as a series, since characters cross over.)
Caught Up in Her (a short prequel novella to Caught Up in Us)
Caught Up in Us
Pretending He's Mine
Trophy Husband
Stars in Their Eyes

Stand-Alone Novels

Big Rock
Mister Orgasm (2016)
Far Too Tempting
21 Stolen Kisses
Playing with Her Heart (a stand-alone Seductive Nights
spin-off novel about Jill and Davis)

The No Regrets Series

The Thrill of It
The Start of Us
Every Second with You

The Seductive Nights Series

Night after Night (Julia and Clay, book one)
After This Night (Julia and Clay, book two)

One More Night (Julia and Clay, book three)
Nights with Him (a stand-alone novel about Michelle and Jack)
Forbidden Nights (a stand-alone novel about Nate and Casey)

The Sinful Nights Series

Sweet Sinful Nights
Sinful Desire
Sinful Longing
Sinful Love

The Fighting Fire Series

Burn for Me (Smith and Jamie)
Melt for Him (Megan and Becker)
Consumed by You (Travis and Cara)

The SAPPHIRE Affair

LAUREN BLAKELY

Montlake
Romance

Published by Montlake Romance, Seattle

www.apub.com

Amazon, the Amazon logo, and Montlake Romance are trademarks of Amazon.com, Inc., or its affiliates.

ISBN-13: 9781503935471
ISBN-10: 1503935477

Cover design by Michael Rehder

Cover photography by Regina Wamba of MaeIDesign.com

Printed in the United States of America

PROLOGUE

Present Day

In truth or dare, everyone knows you should pick dare.

Truth is too risky. It gets you in trouble. But Jake Harlowe had always been drawn to trouble, and maybe, somewhere inside of him, he wanted to tell her the truth.

Even if the truth would lead to more trouble.

As Steph marched to the end of the dock, then spun around, fixing him with a challenging stare, he knew there was only one answer to the question she was about to ask.

"Truth or dare?" she asked, the moonlight framing her stunning, sun-kissed face, the ocean breeze sweeping through her hair, the smell of salt water wrapping around them.

"Truth," he said easily, reaching for his beer bottle and taking a drink as gentle waves lolled past them.

She arched an eyebrow and raised her chin. Her tough-girl stance, and it made her even sexier. Damn, she was hot when she was feisty. "Tell me the truth for real. Did you know who I was the night you met me?"

He scoffed. "I knew you were the hottest woman I'd seen in ages," he said, somehow unable to resist slipping around her question to give her a compliment.

She stared at him. "That's not the whole truth."

"Fine. I knew you were a pain in the ass," he added.

"Gee, thanks."

"I knew you were going to drive me crazy."

"You drive me crazy, too," she countered, parking her hands on her hips.

"Sounds like we're just about even, then."

"No. We're not. Because you still haven't answered the question. Did you know who I was?"

"No," he said, setting his beer on the railing. He stepped closer to her and grasped her bare arms. Her skin was soft and warm. "I've told you a million times. No. No. And more no. And I could ask you the same damn thing, too. I could ask if you knew who I was. But I'm not asking. Because it doesn't matter right now. It doesn't matter anymore." He let go of her arms and gestured from him to her. "This? This isn't about who knew what when. It's about the fact that I can't get you out of my head." He tapped his skull. "It's about the fact that I'm not supposed to get involved on a job. It's about the fact that even if I weren't about to break that rule in spectacular fashion, I should absolutely not break it with you, of all people."

She pressed her teeth into her lower lip, and the tiniest sliver of a smile appeared on her face. Oh hell, he was going to have a field day kissing that smile away all night long and feeling her melt in his arms.

"But you're going to? In spectacular fashion?" she asked, her tone soft and inviting now.

"No more questions, Steph. Your turn is up. It's mine now. So, what'll it be? Truth or dare?"

She licked her lips and raised an eyebrow. "Dare."

Smart woman. She was smarter than he was. Or maybe she just wanted the same thing—a dare to match the truth.

"I dare you to kiss me right now," he said with a grin, knowing she wasn't going to back down, because this woman backed down from absolutely nothing.

She inched closer.

He raised a hand in a stop sign. "I need to give you fair warning. This time, I'm not going to stop at just kissing you."

Her eyes glinted. "You'd better not."

CHAPTER ONE

One Week Earlier...

Any door that didn't put up a fight concerned Jake.

This one in particular was giving off too-good-to-be-true vibes.

As Jake pushed on the heavy green entrance at the edge of the cobblestoned courtyard, still slick from a cold rain this morning, it opened smoothly into the apartment building.

He gave it a side-eye glance.

He was more than ready to use his most reliable tool, a lock-picking kit that he carried with him at all times. Didn't need it now, and that unnerved him. But, given the zigzaggy history of this case so far, maybe the rest of it would be easy all the way.

He'd take easy.

The door creaked shut, leading him to the empty foyer of the tiny building. A row of rusty, once-coppery mailboxes lined the wall, with surnames like Durand and Fournier. Circulars and envelopes lay untouched on the stone floor, having been spit up by too-full boxes. Probably meant the building drew transients. Judging from the dilapidated state of it, that was a good bet. Jake peered up the curving staircase and took the first step, expecting it to groan—not from him, though he was certainly a sturdy, solid man, but from the weight of years. This building had seen a handful of centuries and could probably whisper tales of horse-drawn carriages and blood in the street from the French Revolution.

Watching both his back and the path up, he climbed the steps that were so timeworn they had dips and grooves in them. When he reached the second floor flat that he'd tracked down as the most likely location for the treasure he sought, he stood flush to the wall. From that angle, he had a read on the hallway, the stairs, and the door to the flat. Scanning the surroundings once more for prying eyes or ambushes, he was satisfied he wasn't being watched. He pressed his ear to the door, listening for a cough, a bit of chitchat, any signs of activity.

If the guys were inside the flat, he'd have to improvise. But hell, that was his stock-in-trade. In this line of work, you had to be ready to make it up as you went along. For now, the coast appeared clear. After rapping his knuckles twice on the door just in case, he waited.

Nothing but silence rang in his ears. He surveyed the cramped hallway once more. All was quiet. He removed that handy-dandy lock-picking kit from the back pocket of his jeans, quickly worked open the old French lock, and slipped inside the thimble-size studio apartment. He gagged, covering his mouth with the neck of his gray pullover. The garbage strike in Paris took no prisoners in this home. It reeked of rotten fruit, moldy bread, and unwashed laundry.

He shook his head in disgust. Fucking pigs.

Lowering the neck of his shirt, he did his best to breathe through his mouth as he riffled through a few cupboards and drawers, then spied under the couch.

Nothing but papers, dust bunnies, and bottle caps.

Where could it be? He turned in a tight circle, hunting for nooks, crannies, and hiding places, when he noticed a small bureau in the corner. Clothes were piled high on top of it. Something about the bureau called out to him. Whispered what it might hold inside. His fingertips tingled. He kneeled down, cracked open its doors, and nearly pumped a fist in victory when he spotted the prize.

A gorgeous, glorious Stradivarius.

With a new, long, and unsightly scratch down the body. He narrowed his eyes and clenched his jaw. Bastards didn't even treat something this precious with care.

Reaching for it from amid a mountain of dirty clothes, he gently grasped the neck of the instrument in one hand. Unzipping his backpack, he removed the violin case he'd brought with him, because a goddamn Strad needed to be carried in a padded home. He tucked the rare instrument inside, closed the case, and slid it inside the large backpack. The violin was safe and shielded, and only if you looked closely could you make out the shape of the case pressing against the nylon of the pack, the end of the neck stretching the top.

So be it. No one would get that close to him. That's how he rolled.

Then he heard the sound of voices floating through the window from the courtyard below. Speaking French, but with an Irish accent.

His pulse spiked.

Yup. Don't trust easy. Someone was always lurking around a corner.

Adrenaline surged in him, his veins pumping with the thrill of getting the hell out of Dodge with the prize. He closed the door on the bureau, crossed the five feet in the tiny apartment to the front door, and exited, shutting the door behind him. He adjusted the straps of his pack so the bag hung low on his back. As he headed down the stairs, he grabbed a pair of shades from the front pocket and covered his eyes. *Just an average guy, visiting friends in this building. Nothing more, nothing less.* When he reached the entryway, he strolled straight past the two men as if it were business as usual.

"Nothing but bills," one of them muttered with disdain, grabbing some envelopes from the mailboxes. Their backs were to him.

Hell of a time to be checking the mail. Some might call that a lucky break. Jake certainly did.

He reined in a grin as he made it to the courtyard without them noticing, or seemingly caring about the unknown American in their building, who was walking at an angle to shield the outline of the million-dollar instrument's home. He exhaled, his breath leaving a faint imprint on the chilly air. The men were in his rearview mirror now, probably trudging their way upstairs, where it would take them a few minutes to realize what was missing from their mess.

Served 'em right.

A few minutes was all he needed. A few minutes gave him plenty of time and space and distance. He hoofed it across the courtyard, his gaze fixed on the street ahead, when his boot hit a wet stone.

Squeak.

Like a goddamn burglar alarm.

He winced in frustration from the louder-than-hell sound the sole of his shoe had made. Damn rain.

So much for those minutes he'd been betting on.

The men spun around. One peered at him, narrowed his eyes, then pointed at his back, speaking French in an Irish brogue.

Ah, hell. Guy must have spotted the shape of the instrument.

Jake understood enough French, thanks to having lived overseas. But he didn't need a dictionary to decipher *bloody bastard.* That translated in any language, and those guys wanted the violin on his back.

There was no way in hell he'd let them near it.

He'd been on the trail of the Strad for nearly a month, and had been tracking it here in Paris for a full week. He was prepped and ready to go. He'd paid a taxi driver to wait for him by the curb, so he'd be peeling away from Pigalle any second. Jake didn't need much time to make it to the street, then to his getaway vehicle, then out of the country.

Bon fucking voyage.

He took off, hightailing it around the corner of the courtyard and onto the sidewalk, narrowly sidestepping a trio of already inebriated twentysomethings, who stumbled out of a club with red neon lights that were blinking faintly in the March afternoon. Stopping in his tracks, he scanned for the idling car.

A garbage truck was parked in the spot the cab had nabbed minutes ago, and men were dumping cans of trash in the rear of the vehicle. The cab was gone. *Naturally.* He'd opted for a taxi rather than a car service so there'd be no trail, no name attached. Just his luck that today of all days the garbage strike ended.

Improvise.

He raced nimbly around the drunks, hoping their wobbliness would serve as a roadblock for the guys on his trail. The sound of footsteps intensified, but he continued his assault on the sidewalk, running quickly. Outpacing enemies was second nature. He sped around the corner, darting down a quiet side street that cut across at an odd angle on the way to the edge of Montmartre. Should be easy to grab a taxi there. Slip into a cab, glide into traffic, make the getaway. No need to worry about the first cab; he'd find another, no problem.

But as he curved past a lingerie shop at the end of the block, he stopped short, coming face-to-face with the two men. Mere feet away. *Of course.* They knew this neighborhood better than he did.

The taller of the pair glared at Jake and bared yellowed teeth. "Give back the Strad, and you won't get hurt," he hissed, rolling his *R*s in a way that almost made his threat sound classy, as he brandished a gleaming silver knife.

The blade, though . . . it ruined the sophisticated feel of the moment.

"In theory, that sounds like a fair deal. But I'm going to have to take a pass," Jake said, and swiveled the other way, then flinched as cold, sharp metal dug into his forearm. Oh, that hurt like a son of a bitch, and blood spurted out from his arm. "So, the *bloody bastard* comment? That was literal. Well, so's this," he said, then jammed his elbow in the gut of the yellow-toothed guy. Briefly, Jake clenched his fist, tempted to throw a punishing punch. But even though he could easily land one or many, he wasn't in the mood for a fight. A street brawl would only draw more attention, and right now, he needed less.

As the great Kenny Rogers said, you've got to know when to run.

And when to motherfucking sprint.

Six years in the army served Jake well right now as he sped away, lengthening his stride and barreling past a boisterous scarf-and-coat-wearing and espresso-sipping crowd at a café. The sounds of French chatter about work and politics, art and the news, fell on his ears, and not a single person at the café seemed to care that a man was running like a receiver for the end zone, as red leaked from his forearm.

He gritted his teeth. Damn cut smarted.

A siren blared and Jake cursed. He'd have a hell of a time explaining to the French police that he was simply retrieving a stolen item. *Officer, I know it sure looks like I made off with this priceless instrument, but in reality, I was stealing it back. Yes, I'm a modern-day Robin Hood.* Cops, generally speaking, weren't the friends of men like him, men who were called when the law couldn't or didn't or wouldn't help. He snapped his gaze toward the sound of the siren. Mercifully, the bleating came from a white ambulance. Well, that was good for Jake, bad for whoever was lying on the stretcher inside.

Up ahead, he spied his goal—a busy boulevard, thick with cars and green taxis. He wondered if his disappearing cabbie had come to hunt for fares here.

From behind, the men shouted at him in English as he ran. The red awning of a butcher shop came into view, and the scent of roast chicken from a rotisserie cart parked outside it drifted into his nostrils.

Smelled fantastic. His mouth watered.

If he were in a movie, he'd yank the chicken grill into the middle of the sidewalk and trip the bumbling men, who'd double over in pain as Jake took off into the sunset, leaving them in the dust while nibbling on a tasty cooked chicken. But life wasn't a movie. It was full of risks, and it was up to him to get away with this million-dollar object and return it to his client. No return, no pay. Simple math.

He blasted by a gray-haired French woman in a tweedy skirt and knit hat pushing a shopping bag, as he muttered, *"Excusez-moi."* Then, mere feet away, he spotted a jewel.

Better than an emerald. Prettier than a pile of greenbacks.

A green taxi.

Passengerless and idling at a red light. He sprinted to the door, grabbed the handle, and slid inside.

The cabbie arched a bushy eyebrow. *"Oui?"*

Jake gave the address of his hotel in the seventh arrondissement. Then added in French, *"Quickly, please."*

"How fast?"

"As fast as you can."

"It'll cost you extra."

"Yes. I know," he said drily.

The light changed, and the cab peeled away, leaving two Irish Stradivarius thieves in his wake on the outskirts of Montmartre. His breath came fast as he settled into the backseat, slinging the backpack around to his front. Blood from the knife cut drizzled along his skin. Tugging at the waistband of his shirt, he wiped away the blood. The cut wasn't deep; it was merely a superficial wound.

"You running away from something?" the cab driver asked in French as he tore through side streets toward the Seine.

"No. I don't run away. I'm returning something to its rightful owner."

That was what he did.

Several hours later, his forearm was cleaned up, his shirt had been changed, and the seven-figure violin was safe and sound and heading home. He stepped out of the terminal in Florence, greeted by a gleaming black town car and his client, Francesca Rinaldi, with jet-black corkscrew curls and outstretched arms.

"Do you have it?" she asked, breathless.

"I told you I did," he said, because he'd called her on his way to the airport, telling her he'd tracked it down. For a brief moment on the flight from Paris to Florence, he'd wondered what it would sound like to pluck one of the strings on that violin. He was intrigued, simply because it was a damn Stradivarius and he couldn't help but wonder if it would actually sound like a dull twang after being manhandled by criminals who thought they could get a cool mill for something that everyone knew was missing, or if it would still sound like some kind of siren song, as it was supposed to.

He didn't touch it, though. Not his place. Not his job.

"I want to see it," Francesca said, her eyes wide and eager, her voice desperate and hungry. She placed her palms together, as if praying.

He took off his backpack, unzipped it, and removed the precious object from its special transport. He opened the case and showed her what was inside.

"Oh God, it's perfect," she said, relief in her voice, tears streaming down her cheeks, as she reached for the violin. She brought it to her cheek and sighed happily as she cozied up to it. Just as quickly, she tucked it back inside and gripped the case tightly in her arms. Like a mother holding her once-missing baby. Her gaze landed on his wrist. "You have a cut. Did you get in a fight?"

"I wouldn't call it a fight exactly. But they seemed keen on testing their knife's sharpness on my arm," he said, deadpan.

"A knife!" she shrieked, covering her mouth. "Are you OK?"

He waved off her worry.

Truth be told, the knife had surprised him, given the general level of stupidity the thieves displayed in stealing something that was virtually impossible to fence. That's probably why it had been chucked in a pile of laundry when the scums who stole it realized there was no true black market for a Stradivarius. The two Irish men had lifted this violin from Francesca's niece, a world-renowned musician, at a Dublin train station a few months ago, with dollar signs in their eyes. After trying to peddle the violin in the underground market where not even the most stalwart criminal collectors would touch an item whose provenance was so well-documented, they'd turned to Craigslist to try to pawn it off, and that's how Jake had tracked them down. This hadn't been an easy gig, but it wasn't the toughest job either in his years as a *retrieval expert*. Some called him a private detective, others dubbed him a bounty hunter, and sure, technically, he was that, too. Most of the assignments were to hunt down goods—usually precious objects, and every now and then he'd need to find a person. So, *retrieval expert* seemed to work as a catchall title.

Francesca preferred to call him a bounty hunter.

"Do you need a Band-Aid?"

Jake shook his head and laughed. "I don't do Band-Aids."

"Why not? Not rugged enough?" she asked with a playful pout.

"Exactly. No one wants to hire a bounty hunter sporting a Band-Aid."

Francesca wrapped a hand around his arm, gently stroking near the cut but careful not to touch. "You're right. We like you rugged. And I cannot thank you enough for finding this precious object. I'm so very grateful. This means the world to us," she said, then reached for her phone and tapped it a few times. "There. I just wired you the fee." He nodded a thanks. "Now, would you like to come and hear Arianna play it tomorrow night? We are setting up a private concert on the veranda of my villa to celebrate the return of the Stradivarius. You will be our guest of honor." She leaned in closer and lowered her voice. "The weather is much better here than in Paris. Say you'll stay."

Her eyes seemed to twinkle with hopefulness and the sliver of a suggestion that perhaps he'd stay for more than the weather, more than the music.

He blinked, then swallowed.

Perhaps he was reading too much into the way she'd inched closer. Regardless, Jake didn't even entertain the possibilities of getting involved with a client. There were lines. Those lines needed to be maintained to run a clean business, and business paid all those bills that he was responsible for. So. Many. Bills.

Besides, home was calling his name.

"Ah, I wish I could. But I need to head back. See my family."

"You are a good family man."

"I do what I can," he said with an *it's-nothing* shrug, even though his sisters and brother were everything to him. He nodded to the instrument. "'Fraid to tell you, the violin might need a Band-Aid. It has a scratch on it."

She held up a hand and shook her head. "Do not worry. I have a restorer on standby. We will fix it."

"By the way, you might want to tell your niece not to take the train anymore with her million-dollar violin. Maybe opt for a taxi next time she finishes a solo performance at the National Concert Hall in Dublin," he quipped as he slung his backpack on his shoulder, ready to turn around and head inside to book a flight home. He kept his returns open-ended, preferring to make game-day decisions since he never knew how long a job would take. "Though, honestly, cabs aren't always a better bet."

Francesca laughed deeply. "If only she would listen to me. She is so independent and stubborn."

He laughed, too. "Young people are like that."

She parked a hand on her hip and wagged a finger at him. "Speaking of stubborn, why didn't you let me fly you here from Paris? I have a jet, you know. I would have been happy to let you use it."

"Nah. Commercial works fine for me."

"I insist you take it home, then."

He shot her a look that said she was crazy. Home was far away. "All the way to Miami?"

She nodded vigorously. "I'm sending my plane there anyway. It's being serviced nearby. Take it. Please. Think of it as a tip. Hazard pay."

Jake raised an eyebrow. Sometimes the job had its perks. He didn't mind those at all, especially if the plane was making its way over the Atlantic already . . .

"It comes with an open bar. And your favorite Scotch," she said, sweetening the pot. Ah, it was good to have clients like Francesca who liked to reward those who worked for her.

"I believe you've just convinced me," he said, and took off for the airport where a private plane awaited him.

Somewhere over Spain, with the jet softly humming in his ears, the blue skies painting the world beyond the windows, and the Scotch tasting like the best medicine there ever was, Jake put up his feet and took a long nap.

∽♋

When he touched down in his hometown, he rubbed his eyes, stretched his arms, ran a hand through his messy brown hair, and mapped out his day. He wasn't even sure what day of the week it was, or what time, either. But it was warm and sunny, and that was all he needed to refuel after more than a week on the road. He was looking forward to going for a run on the beach, then taking his nephew, Mason, for a bike ride, then a day of fishing with his little brother, Brandt, when he came home for spring break from his final year of college.

As he stepped off the jet and onto the tarmac, his phone buzzed. His sister was calling.

"Jake," she said as soon as he answered. "Are you back?"

"Obviously, I just answered the phone. Doesn't ring in the sky, Kate."

He could practically see her roll her eyes. "Ha ha ha. Don't get too comfy. We have another job."

He groaned. Sure, he was grateful for the work. But a little down-time before he caught another flight would be nice.

"This is easy. All you have to do is find a guy who's barely trying to hide."

But nothing was ever easy. "Tell me more about the job."

"It includes one of your favorite things ever."

"A day on the boat? Season tickets to the Marlins? A cold beer and barbecue?"

"Try beaches full of hot women in bikinis all day long."

More like his greatest temptation.

CHAPTER TWO

A school of fish so blue they shimmered like jewels swam past her, stirring up the crystal-clear water with dainty little ripples. One of the fish darted so close that its fins brushed against Steph's leg, making her laugh silently. With the regulator in her mouth, she turned to her brother and waved to the underwater camera he held.

The Miami sun from high above them was like a faint spotlight, offering flickers of bright little rays off the coast of South Beach. Steph resumed her path through the sunset-pink reef, darting by plants that danced and swayed in the sea, tranquil and gorgeously silent.

She kicked her legs and swam alongside the blue tang fish as they cut past the living rock. Their scales glittered like sapphires. Breathing in through the regulator, she bobbed near the fish, enjoying the calm sensation of being at one with the natural world. Playing in it. But leaving it as it was.

Perfect advertisement for her business . . . which still needed the help.

About the only thing that would sell better than fish would be if she found a pirate's buried treasure beneath the sea. She imagined uncovering a rusty old wooden box, bursting with hidden gems. Once upon a time, she'd dreamed of uncovering such a find in the sea. Hunting through shipwrecks in search of long-lost gold. Absently, she fingered the chain around her neck with its mini treasure chest on it.

As she skimmed near the sandy bottom of this shallow ledge, a dazzling pair of purple parrot fish shot past her, racing into an underground cavern too narrow for humans. Her eyes lit up, and her excitement was surely visible as she glanced back at the camera pointing to the neon fish, one of the most coveted sights on a dive.

They were, quite simply, stunning.

The ocean's true treasure chest—the beautiful creatures that called it home. After the parrot fish disappeared in the cavern, her work was done. She made a circular sign with her hand. *It's a wrap.*

Soon she and her brother, Robert, shot up through the water. The moment of reentry was always thrilling, shifting from surviving underwater for thirty minutes to breathing that fabulous concoction known as air.

As she broke the surface, it was as if hearing had been restored. A pelican squawked as it soared from out of nowhere and dipped into the ocean, hunting for fish. The gentle sound of waves pulsing toward the shore landed on her ears. The sun beat down, and the world was bright again, replacing the dark serenity of the underwater realm. Steph adored both worlds—the air and the sea, loving that she could live in one and at least exist in the other, thanks to all this awesome gear.

Robert surfaced next, tugged off his mask, and gave a thumbs-up.

"Great footage," he said. "The parrot fish rocked it."

"Thanks. I rehearsed them in advance."

"Excellent. You've got them on payroll now?"

She swam to the boat, shouting, "Yup. Blue tang and parrot fish do my bidding. Dolphins next. They drive a harder bargain, but they'll be jumping above the water later, like Flipper. I promised them tuna," she said in a pretend whisper.

"Just let me know when their call time is and I'll be here, Ariel."

She laughed as he used her childhood nickname, the one her mom had bestowed on her on an island vacation long ago. The one she gave to her business when she changed its name last year. Because she *had* to.

Steph reached for a hand at the edge of the boat. Locking fingers with Lance, her longtime friend who ran day fishing tours, she hoisted herself onto the vessel. Robert followed. Never leave a private boat alone or unmoored while diving. You might become shark bait or just have to swim for a really long time to land. Steph was a water girl through and through, but neither option sounded appealing, especially the one that involved becoming lunch, so Lance had manned the boat as they filmed underwater videos to advertise Ariel's Island Eco-Adventure Tours. All part of the rebuilding process, and she was grateful to have their help. They quickly removed their dive gear and stowed it away. Robert, a professional photographer, set down his camera.

"Get what you wanted?" Lance asked. He held up a hand and flashed his sparkling grin that made his smile catnip for many women. "Wait. That was a dumb question. You always get what you want."

"Hardly," Steph said with a scoff because she worked her butt off for everything she had.

"Let me amend that. The new Steph gets what she wants"—he pointed at her—"because she takes no prisoners."

She nodded. "Yes, that's the new me. Merciless," she said, adopting a tough glower.

"More like determined," Robert weighed in. As Lance turned the key in the ignition, they sped toward land, the skyline of South Beach in their crosshairs.

Her wet hair whipped behind her as they cut through the waves, and this was heaven for Steph. Working outdoors. If she never spent a night inside, she'd be the happiest woman alive. The sun, the sand, the surf. The mountains, the hikes, the trails. Bliss—all of it. She'd almost lost her business more than a year ago, but thanks to her mother's help, she'd started anew.

As they reached the marina, Lance slowed the motor, navigating through other sailors returning to the beach.

"When do you leave for your next adventure tour?" Robert asked.

She rubbed her hands together. "I'm so excited for this one. I'm running a rock climbing and dive gig in the Caymans."

"Nice. First job there in a while, right?"

Nodding, she twisted her index and middle finger together. "Took me *months* to get this one," she said, letting out a long breath, because it felt like she'd been holding it forever as she waited for the tour to come through. The Caymans were hit the hardest in her ex-boyfriend Duke's slash-and-burn. "Then I head to Turks and Caicos for a private tour there. And that gives *you* plenty of time to cut the video and post it on the site before I leave," she said, batting her eyes and adopting a wide smile, even though Robert was well aware that she wanted to use the footage to advertise her tour company's growing work in vacation spots around the equator, starting with her home base of Miami and spanning across the Caribbean from the Caymans to Aruba to the Bahamas. "And I can book some Miami dives for when I return."

Robert rolled his light-blue eyes and ran a hand through his hair, golden from years in the sun, like hers. "Always working."

"When work is play, it's hardly work," she tossed back. "Besides, it sure beats *not* working, and I had enough of that in the past year to last a lifetime."

He raised a closed fist and knocked it against hers. "Here's to keeping busy and saying fuck you to the asshole who tried to tank you," he said as he parked a foot on the dash. "And anytime you need me to shoot something for you, I'll gladly do it."

"I'll second that. Well, when it comes to driving the boat," Lance called out, then did a double take, narrowing his dark eyes at Robert. "Hey, get your stinky foot off my dashboard."

Steph leaned forward to pretend to wipe the dash. "Don't worry, Lance. I'll clean it up for you. I want *Sally* to look pretty, too," she said, patting the boat as she used the name he'd given it long ago—the shaggy mutt he'd had as a kid. "See you in a couple hours, Captain," she said with a salute, then helped moor *Sally* to the dock.

"Amen to that," Lance said.

When they were done, she said good-bye to her brother and her friend, then hopped into her red car, lowered the top, and headed up the road to the South Beach main drag. Once in town, she parked a block away from her mom's favorite fish taco restaurant and met her mother, Shelly, for a cocktail at the street-side bar. Well, mocktails for Steph, since she had more work to do—leading a sunset snorkel trip off Key Biscayne in a few hours—and she'd made sure to hire Lance as her crew for that one. One way of saying thanks for how he'd helped her, she made sure she sent all her new business in Miami to her buddy.

"You're too tan, sweetheart. You need to wear sunscreen. Or a hat," her mother said, gesturing to her own wide-brimmed hat that was large enough to provide a landing pad for creatures from outer space. She wore yoga pants, a sports bra, and a silvery necklace she'd made herself. It matched the one Steph wore.

"The tan is kind of an occupational hazard," Steph said, gesturing to her getup—green bikini covered by blue swim shorts and a loose tank. "I can slather myself with the stuff, but even then, the sun leaves its mark," she added as the waiter brought the drinks—virgin piña colada for Steph and a mojito for her mom.

They had a standing afternoon get-together every Monday and Thursday. Her mother was strong and didn't like to let on how lonely she'd been since her divorce from Steph's stepfather two years ago after nearly two decades of marriage and raising her two kids with him. But the twice-a-week meetings told Steph that yoga classes and a return to work hadn't filled the void yet. Steph felt that void, too, though she'd never admit that to her mom. She missed the now-defunct holiday get-togethers, the occasional picnics at the beach, and especially the times when the three of them would grab lunch together at an outdoor café and she'd share stories from her adventure trips.

"Slather yourself more," her mother said, issuing it like a *clean-your-room* instruction, even though Steph was twenty-eight and had long since outgrown such directives. Besides, her room was quite neat, thank you very much. Her whole condo was. Kicking out her ex had done wonders for the cleanliness level of her place. The man had been a slob, but all things considered, that was one of the nicest things she could say about Duke.

"I will," Steph said, even though she probably wouldn't, but her mom liked to keep busy, and busy meant doling out parental advice, so Steph went along with it.

As her mom brought the glass to her lips, she tipped her forehead to the sidewalk. "Incoming hotness at two p.m.," her mom whispered out of the corner of her lips.

"Mom," Steph admonished.

"Not for me. For you. You deserve a little fun. Look," she urged.

Steph shook her head but took the bait, because hotness was hard to resist checking out. She followed her mom's gaze and nearly murmured her approval out loud when her eyes landed on a tall, trim, and dark-haired man in tan slacks, a crisp white button-down, and aviator shades. His jaw was chiseled, dusted with the perfect amount of stubble, and his lips looked oh-so-kissable.

Kissing. Hmm. What was that? Just a hazy blur. Steph had to reach far back in the mental files to remember.

"Whoa," she whispered under her breath.

"Talk to him," her mom said in a quiet voice, nudging Steph with an elbow. "He probably likes you, too."

OK, time to nip this one in the bud. No matter how smoking hot he was, nor how long it had been since Steph's body had been held against the opposite sex, she was *not* going to proposition a stranger walking down the street. She lowered her shades and turned to her mom.

"Yes, he's hot. But let's break this down. One, he doesn't like me. He doesn't know me. He's walking down the street. That's not an indication of his interest in me. That's a sign of his *direction*. He probably has a meeting that way," she said, waving her arm in the direction of the gorgeous businessman. "And two, even if he had been checking me out, which he was not, I'm not going to go race after some guy on the street and say, '*Hi, you're cute, want to go out?*' And three, I have no time in my life for men. And four, hello! Have you forgotten? Men are trouble."

Her mom laughed loudly, with her straight, white teeth showing. It was nice to see her smile. "Fine, the last one might be true," her mom said. "But don't you think it's time you ended the moratorium? It's been a year." She dropped a hand on Steph's arm, squeezing gently.

More like two years, three months, and nine days.

"And it's taken that long to erase the damage Duke did," Steph said, then softened her gaze. "Thanks to you. None of what I've accomplished would have been possible without your help."

Her mom waved a hand in the air, as if to say it was nothing. When, in fact, her mom's wisdom, insight, and savvy had been *everything*. She'd saved Steph's business from near ruin when Duke had slammed her professional reputation online after their breakup. "You know I'd do anything for you. Including encourage you to pick up hot men on the street," she said with a wink, then gestured to the throngs of tourists and locals streaming by. "Let's people watch."

One of Steph's favorite pastimes. As they sipped their beverages, they made up wild tales about the crazy getups they saw, from a man in spangly silver shorts to a woman with only a painted-on bikini—literally, it was made of paint. When the bill came, her mother grabbed it quickly.

"Mom, it's my treat," Steph said, trying to snatch it away, wanting to help out her mom.

Her mother held the check high in the air. "You'll do no such thing."

"Please," she said, adopting a puppy smile and wide eyes. She wasn't privy to the full state of her mother's finances, but she knew they'd changed drastically since the split. After years of mostly being a stay-at-home parent, she'd returned to selling jewelry at craft fairs. *Spending money*, her mom had called it. Lack of alimony was another term that worked. *Royally screwed* fit, too.

Her mother shook her head and held the bill far out of reach. "It's all mine. I had a good week at my table at the Miami Beach fair."

"Next time it's on me. I insist," Steph said, since her business was growing again.

"We'll see if I let you pay next time, too," her mom said, handing the money to the waitress, then returning her focus to Steph. "Oh, I nearly forgot. I heard a little something about Eli and his nightclub business," she said, her voice dripping with disdain as she mentioned her ex-husband.

Steph's shoulders tightened, because these days her feelings for Eli were complicated. While she despised that he'd cheated on her mom and shredded her heart, the little girl in her couldn't help still loving the only father she'd ever really known. Her own father died of a heart attack when she was three and Robert was four. That was why this internal tug-of-war hurt so much—it was a damn shame that Eli had been such a crummy husband, because he was never a lousy father. He'd been good to Steph her whole life. It was as if he were two men—the good dad she knew and the terrible husband her mother was more familiar with.

Steph raised an eyebrow. "What did you hear?"

"Andrew called. One of his former business partners."

"This is the Andrew I did a dive tour for a few years back? Your old school friend?" Steph continued, making sure she was remembering the details.

Her mom adjusted her necklace and nodded. "Right. I introduced him to Eli when he needed someone with his skills, and I knew Andrew would be perfect. Anyway, Andrew has been trying to reach him, but he's too busy in the Caymans with his new fiancée and his new club, *Sapphire*," she said, narrowing her eyes as she breathed the name like it cost her something. "And I might as well have paid for that damn club. Because Andrew thinks Eli might have used money he stole from the business to start it up."

Steph's jaw dropped. That was taking underhanded to a whole new level. But Eli didn't mess around when it came to his wants and wishes. The thought immediately hit her with a fresh wave of sadness. For a while, making Steph feel happy and loved had been part of those wishes. But that was a long time ago.

"Are you kidding me?" she asked her mom. If only it really were a bad joke.

Steph's mom held her arms out wide. "That's what they said. They're looking into it and trying to figure out where the money the firm invested in a mysterious cocoa bean farm went," she said, taking a final sip of her mojito.

"Into his nightclub in the Caymans?"

"Supposedly. They might send someone down there to look into it. Hey! I have an idea!" Her mom lowered her voice to a conspiratorial whisper. "Can you lift his Rolex if you happen to see him next time you're there?"

Steph laughed and draped an arm around her mom's shoulder. "Gladly. He loves that stupid Rolex. If you teach me how to pickpocket, Mom, I'll bring that watch back for you, no questions asked." Steph grabbed her purse and slung it on her shoulder. "Actually," she said as an idea took hold. "I'm going there for a tour this week."

Her mom laughed as she set down her emptied drink. "You don't have to steal his watch, sweetie."

"No, but maybe I can find out a little bit more about the club and the money. I haven't been there in several months, since the last time I saw him, but I still know a ton of people. I'll ask around."

Steph's mom shot her a stern stare. "Focus on your tour. Not him. Besides, enough about him. Talking about my ex too much is bad for my chakra," her mother said, tapping her heart. "That's what my yoga guru would say. I need to focus on the path in front of me," she said, pointing into the distance, as if to prove that she wasn't caught up in the past. "Not the douchenozzle in my past who tried to bleed every last penny from me." Her mother clasped her hand over her mouth. "I'm sorry," she said, dropping her hand. "I shouldn't talk about your stepdad that way."

"It's OK. Sometimes you have to unleash the anti-chakra sentiments," Steph said with a grin. She may not want to believe Eli could do something so terrible, but she'd never fault her mom for a little smack talk against the man who broke her heart.

Her mom shook her head. "Nope. I need to be a better person. Holding on to the past interferes with my prana. Or something like that."

"Yeah. Something like that indeed," Steph muttered, or maybe the prana needed someone to run interference.

For far too long, Steph wasn't able to do a damn thing about her stepdad's straying ways. She couldn't stop his wandering, of course, and she couldn't make him a better husband, nor could she convince him to play fair in the divorce, though she'd tried, begging him at times to back down. He was like a different person, though, when it came to matters of the heart, and it cut her to the core to see how the same man who'd taught her how to swim, how to multiply fractions, and how to change the tire on a car had turned a deaf ear to her when it came to her pleas about the divorce.

She'd seen her mom give everything for love—her heart, her time, and her money, since she'd given him the funds he needed to start his firm many years ago. The money was a gift; her mom had wanted to help make his dreams come true.

For him to turn around and battle so coldly to keep everything when they split had hollowed out Steph's insides.

Her chest burned with frustration over how he'd hurt the one person he was supposed to adore, then took her for everything he could get his hands on. Fine, both Eli and her mom had said their feelings for Steph and Robert were totally separate from their marriage, and perhaps that was true. But it was also true that even a happy family could fall apart, and that was just more proof to her that her mother was right—all men were trouble.

After she said good-bye and led a sunset dive that her customers said was one of their Miami vacation highlights—a sentiment that warmed her heart—Steph changed her flight to the Caymans. A few extra days on the front end, and she'd use that time to do some digging.

It might be a long shot, but maybe, just maybe, Eli hadn't stolen to start his club. Maybe some shred of the man she loved like a father still existed and this was some sort of misunderstanding. Money matters were complicated, after all.

And if he had taken what wasn't his, perhaps he'd respond to a logical, polite, heartfelt plea to do the right thing. Especially if she was the one to deliver that plea. She'd been his soft spot growing up. Maybe she still could be now.

But if it turned out he'd taken what wasn't his, then she'd kick this damn hope to the curb and fight like hell to get her mother's money back.

Because you just can't let the bastards get away with everything.

CHAPTER THREE

Art, a tropical island, and some bad chocolate. That's what Jake's next gig was all about.

Crying shame, since chocolate should only be good.

"Let me get this straight. You think Eli put the stolen money from chocolate investments gone wrong into art, and took that art out of the country?"

His client nodded. "It's easier to move art than money."

Jake scratched his chin. "Another question. Chocolate is an actual investment? Should I be buying up Godiva now? Scharffen Berger?" Jake arched an eyebrow as he took off his shades. He looked Andrew in the eyes as the sun cast golden rays on the Key Largo boardwalk. Andrew had driven down from Miami where he was based and hadn't even balked when Jake moved the location of their meeting from his office to the boardwalk at midday. The gray-haired man was dressed in slacks and a button-down. Jake was dressed for a dip in the water with his nephew when they were done.

"Cocoa beans are a commodity," Andrew said, wiping a big paw across his sweaty forehead. He had a manila envelope tucked under his arm. "Apparently, cocoa beans are the new coconuts. Or so we thought."

"Like that coconut water crap?" Jake asked as he peered down the boardwalk to make sure Mason didn't get too far away on his bike. His nephew pedaled past a sandwich shop. "I mean, *Mother Nature's sports drink*," he said in mock seriousness. "What's next? Chocolate water that makes you healthier?"

Andrew rolled his eyes. "Don't even get me started. I tried that coconut water diet and it did nothing for me. Hoping it would have taken ten pounds off the old flat tire here, but no such luck." He patted his stomach, then pointed to Jake. "But you, I'm sure you don't have to worry about that."

Jake simply shrugged. No flat tires allowed here, but this meeting wasn't about diet crazes or the best way to stay in shape. It was about whether Jake could help Andrew and his screwed-over business partner.

He hung his shades on the neck of his T-shirt. "So you're saying Eli Thompson, who started the Eli Fund twenty years ago, with money his then-wife gave him from sales of her craft fair coral necklace jewelry, so he could launch a hedge fund for '*Bob in Middle America*,'" Jake said, stopping to sketch air quotes as he used the term Eli himself bandied about in the marketing of his investment firm, "has been skimming pennies off the top for years?"

"Yup. And you know what happens to lots of pennies over time?"

"I'm going to go out on a limb here. Do they turn into dollars? And then do those dollars become Benjamins and so on?" He made a rolling gesture with his hand.

Andrew tapped his nose. "Bingo."

Jake peered down the boardwalk. "Mason!" he shouted to his sister's kid, who was speeding off in the distance. "Don't go past the ice-cream shop. That's too far."

"Ten bucks says that's probably where he's headed," Andrew said with a smile.

"Double or nothing says you're right," Jake said, then started walking in Mason's direction. His nephew had just learned to ride a bike after a few solid months of practice. The kid was a natural now, but he was embracing his freedom a little too quickly for his uncle's taste. With flip-flops slapping on the sidewalk, Jake quickened his pace. "Be right back," he said to his potential client. Seconds later, Mason turned around and grinned wildly.

"Did you see how far I rode?" Mason shouted from many feet away.

"I did. And it was so far you started to turn into a speck. And a speck of Mason is too small, so stay closer," Jake said, drawing a circle with his index finger as Mason rode to him. "If you do, we'll get the chocolate peanut-butter-cup scoop, 'K?"

"My favorite!"

"Mine, too, buddy. Mine, too," he said, and Jake was already looking forward to an ice-cream cone. That'd be his reward for a potential new business deal. Ice cream—now that'd be an investment worth making. Ice cream never went out of style. Come to think of it, Jake might invest in some Ben & Jerry's. Or Talenti. That was some seriously good stuff. Ice cream was his guilty pleasure, and since working out was his best friend, he never truly felt guilty.

"I'll stay closer," Mason said, the smile never leaving his face as he pedaled in the other direction.

Jake walked back to Andrew, returning his focus to the conversation as they leaned against the boardwalk fence. "How much money are we talking?"

"About ten million." Andrew shook his head in disgust.

He whistled. "Damn. Skimming is a hot business these days. I made the wrong career choice for getting rich," he joked.

"You and me both."

Jake raised his chin, returning to his serious mode. "I need to ask—how did you have no idea this was happening? You and your brother, Aaron, are Eli's right-hand men in the fund, you said. Was this all under your nose?" He aimed to be direct with clients. Going into work armed with facts was the only way to operate.

"Unfortunately, yes. But we all have different areas of expertise." Andrew tapped his chest. "That's how we split up the work, so we could make bets in different areas. Lots of those bets don't pay off—that's the nature of a hedge fund. But when the cocoa bean farm went belly-up at the same time Eli retired to the Caymans sooner than we expected him to, that's when we started thinking there might be a pattern," he offered, then heaved a deep sigh, flubbing his lips. "Wish I'd caught on to this sooner. Makes me feel stupid not to have checked before."

"Hey now," Jake said, trying to reassure the guy. "Don't beat yourself up. Just give me the details."

Mason wheeled to a stop by Jake's side, the brakes braying loudly. "See! I'm going to be a cycling pro like my dad," he said, then started up again, and Jake fixed on a smile for Mason, not wanting to breathe a negative word about the kid's deadbeat dad, who was hardly a cycling pro. More like a bum—a cycling groupie who followed the pros around as they raced in Europe, spending more time with them than his own kid who he hadn't seen in a year.

Mason took off in the other direction, and Jake locked eyes with Andrew once more. "My sister's at a parent-teacher conference," he said, explaining.

"Hey, no worries. I've got three of my own," Andrew said.

"Anyway, so what did you find out? I want to understand as much as I can if I'm going to take this on."

Andrew took a deep breath, then explained how Eli funneled a bit of dough each year into odd investments that didn't pan out, pocketing the money, bit by bit so the other partners wouldn't notice. "The most recent one was the cocoa bean farm. Once that went bust, he retired to the Caymans and opened a nightclub. Ergo . . ." Andrew let his voice trail off with the obvious.

"Ah, the Caymans. The haven of money fraud." Jake crossed his arms. "OK, fine. So he supposedly embezzled all this money over the years from these little hidden investments."

Another nod. "We believe that's what happened."

Jake blew out a long stream of air. "That's a pretty serious allegation. Got any proof?"

Three simple words, but they meant everything right now. No way was Jake going into this situation without some hard evidence.

Andrew nodded and tapped the manila folder he'd brought with him. "We started digging into his files. His e-mails. Anything we could find from the servers. He was pretty thorough in covering his trail, but our IT forensics team was able to track down a few unusual e-mails. Some we're still sorting through, but one of them includes a deleted e-mail from Eli to Constantine Trevino," he said, and Jake's eyebrows drew together.

Jake knew the name. Everyone in his line of work—recovering stolen goods—knew the name. Need art moved illegally? You called Constantine. Want blood diamonds? He was your guy. Hankering for some ivory tusks? Constantine was the middleman.

"The luxury-goods trafficker," Jake said as Andrew unfastened the clasp on the envelope. "I know of him. He can move anything."

"Evidently. That's why our radar went off. In this e-mail, Eli references a payment for ten million dollars. That's the amount that's missing. Well, to be precise, it was $10,003,597. We can document that as the money that's missing from the investments in the fund over the last five years. It was incredibly calculated as far as I can see. The missing money over time added up to the money cited in this transaction, which also references the need for *safe transport, for a grand*."

Andrew handed him the paperwork. Jake read the e-mail carefully, as well as the related documents. That was some damning evidence right there in black and white, but Jake still wanted his sister Kate to vet it. In the years since he'd started this business, she'd developed and honed her expertise in all sorts of document verification, and he relied on her eyes and her analytical mind to confirm that the evidence added up. What Jake brought to the table, besides the on-the-ground work, was his possession of an excellent bullshit detector, and so far it wasn't ringing in concern. The man seemed legit.

"You have digital copies, too?" he asked, handing the papers to Andrew.

"Yes. I can send them over immediately."

"You said you think the ten million he embezzled from the fund went into art. Into a painting. Why art?"

"His fiancée runs an art gallery that sells high-end art to discerning buyers in the Cayman Islands. And," Andrew said, taking a beat, "because art is portable and it requires *safe transport.*"

"For a grand?"

"Evidently."

Jake nodded, letting the details soak in, from the amount, to the parties involved, to the methodical level of planning.

"Question for you. Tell me why I should care. Tell me why I should get on a plane and go to the Caribbean and track down your guy and his painting. Tell me something other than the fee you're going to pay me. Because money isn't my only motivation. I need to know why this matters."

Jake had nothing against money, and he definitely enjoyed the way dollars he earned paid for college for his younger brother, Brandt, who was applying to law school, and his little sister, Kylie. The baby of the family, she'd been struggling in a few classes but, fingers crossed, was starting to turn her grades around. But he wasn't in this line of business for the greenbacks.

He was in it because he craved the chance to right a wrong.

"Here's why," Andrew said, rolling up his shirtsleeves. "The whole average Joe and Bob in Middle America approach of our firm? That's true. That's who we serve. We built this company with Eli on the premise of making a hedge fund accessible to the guy who runs a body shop in Ohio or to the woman who operates her own booth at a hair salon. Real people, saving money for retirement, saving the money for their kids' college funds." That hit close to home, making Jake's chest twinge with both anger and memories. His parents had been Middle Americans through and through. Dad was a retired cop in Tampa, and Mom had worked in dispatch. They'd been tucking money aside for both causes and never had the chance to see either retirement or any of their four kids go to college—not Kate, not Jake, and not the two younger ones, Brandt and Kylie.

"Those are the people who got screwed by Eli's cocoa bean farm that didn't pan out," Andrew said, jabbing his finger against the wood post. "I don't care if you get the money back for me. I truly don't. I'll survive just fine. But I do care about the hairdresser. And I do care about the mechanic. And I do care that Eli 'Cocoa-Beans-are-the-New-Coconut-Water' Thompson made off with their money. We want to locate the painting, or paintings, he bought with the fund's money, sell the art through legitimate channels, and put the money back into the fund. This is the rightful property of the Eli Fund, not the rightful property of Eli Thompson."

That was compelling enough, but Jake had more questions, similar to ones he'd ask any client. "Why not go to the cops? The SEC?"

"We're a private firm, so it's not an SEC matter. Plus, we want to see if we can resolve this as quietly as possible, keep our existing clients, and restore the money to them."

"Send me the paperwork today. Kate will handle it and we'll get back to you with a decision," he said.

Andrew grabbed his cell phone from his back pocket. "I've got it all in a draft for you. On its way to you and Kate," he said, swiping the screen.

Jake nodded a thanks, then held up a finger. "One more thing. If there's a raisin grove in Jamaica I'm thinking of putting some cash into," he said, stroking his chin as if in deep thought, "would you tell me that's a bad idea? My financial advisor wants me to drop a cool grand into it. Says raisins are the new grapefruit diet," he said, keeping a straight face.

Andrew eyed him seriously for a split second, then cracked up, pointing playfully at Jake. "You almost had me there for a second. You really had me. And, by the way, the answer is yes. Raisins are a very bad idea."

After Andrew left, Jake and Mason played in the waves for a bit.

"Want to get some raisin ice cream?" Jake asked his nephew as they toweled off.

Mason crinkled his nose. "Eww."

"How about fig sherbet?"

The kid laughed and shook his head.

"I know. Why don't we try chia seed gelato?"

"Gross!"

"Fine, fine," Jake said, pretending to relent as they headed to grab chocolate peanut-butter-cup cones. By the time he returned to the office two hours later, with a conked-out Mason sound asleep in his arms, Kate said everything from Andrew checked out, so Jake booked the next flight to the Caymans.

"What did you learn about Eli Thompson?" he asked his sister as Mason snoozed on the couch in the corner of the office.

"He studied art history in college before he moved into finance. His fiancée has made some pretty impressive art deals over the years," Kate said, her blue eyes as fierce as he'd ever seen them. Kate shared the same drive, the same motivation as Jake. No surprise there. She'd practically raised Jake and the younger siblings after their parents were killed in a car crash when he and Kate were teenagers. "Her name is Isla, and the gallery she runs is pretty classy. I checked out its location. There's a bar down the block from the art gallery she works out of if you want to stop in and ask around."

"Always start at a bar," he quipped.

"You might meet a pretty woman in a bikini there, too," she said, wiggling her eyebrows. Typical Kate—she wanted to play matchmaker for him. A nudge here, a push there, and she was sure she'd have Jake at the altar. Not likely.

He scoffed. "Not going to the Caymans to pick up women at bars."

"Then maybe the beach," Kate added, egging him on.

"Not there, either."

"You need to check out his club, too. See if there's a connection between the money, the art, and the club. And"—she mimed dancing—"maybe you'll do a little dirty dancing with a nice island gal."

"Get out of here. Work and women don't mix and you know that," he said, and there was a damn good reason for that golden rule. He'd made the foolish mistake a few years ago of getting involved on a job with a stunning brunette named Rosalinda with a penchant for high heels. He'd been on the trail of a stolen Medici artifact in Venice that had been lifted in a larger heist. She was on the hunt for a different piece of the collection, so they'd joined forces, formed an ad hoc business partnership on one of the biggest gigs he'd ever had—it spanned months, and cities, and many hotel bedrooms where they'd spent their nights together.

Until the day he finally got his hands on the artifact, and she stole it from under his nose that evening. His jaw clenched as he remembered the way it felt to have been played like that. Turned out she'd been working with some big criminal syndicate that was trying to steal the entire collection. Good thing he was smarter and faster than she was, and he'd learned her habits and weaknesses. He'd managed to catch up to her in a shoe boutique, of all places, and steal it back on behalf of his clients, the rightful owners.

Taught him a damn good lesson, though.

Don't get involved on a job. There was too much on the line.

His livelihood. His family's well-being. He took care of all of the Harlowes through this job, and no woman was worth that risk.

Especially a backstabbing thief of a woman.

These days, his focus was work and only work. That's exactly what he intended to do in the Caymans. Nothing would get in his way.

CHAPTER FOUR

Ah, dive bars were the best.

Pink Pelican rocked that vibe like nobody's business. He could picture this spot fitting in perfectly in Key Largo. Hell, he could practically be in the Keys right now. The wood walls were lined with seashells. Jack Johnson played from a stereo system. A dartboard hung on a wall at the far side of the joint. The whole place smelled of beer.

Translation: heaven.

Add in the talkative Marie, and this stop had been nothing but good news. The bartender with a long mess of brown hair braided tightly was friendly and chatty. With a few well-placed questions that didn't give him away, he learned some key details about the nightclub at the end of the block—info that couldn't be gleaned online. Jake would visit it later when the moon rose high in the sky and see if he could get a bead on whether Eli was hiding his art there. Hell, the guy might have turned the art into cash already and fed those greenbacks into the club.

Either way, he couldn't sniff around now at five in the evening. Stopping by a club at this early-bird hour would make him stick out like a sore thumb, so it was break time. Blending in was essential on a job like this on a small island, and Jake did his best to look like a man on vacation in the Caymans. He'd contemplated playing the part of the finance man, but he didn't seem like a guy who worked in the shade. He was a man who worked in the sun, so he'd decided on the easiest cover-up of all—one that could be true. He was thirty-year-old Jake Harlowe, former soldier, now in the "recovery" business, and here on a fishing trip with his buddies. Marie was an avid fisherwoman, so they'd exchanged tales of the ones they'd caught and the ones that had gotten away.

"Tomorrow should be a great day on the water," Marie said as she wiped the counter. "I bet you'll have a fantastic haul. Marlins and groupers galore."

"Excellent. That's what I want to hear."

"What else will you do while in town? Snorkel trip? Dive? Stingray kiss?"

He arched an eyebrow at the last one but quickly answered her, resting his elbows on the bar. "Let me tell you something. I've always wanted some island art. Gonna just come right out and admit it," he said, as if he were confessing, even though he was clearly teasing. "It's kinda like a thing of mine. Some painting of a fish jumping out of the water," he said, gesturing to the right, to indicate the art gallery run by Eli's new woman. He'd wandered past it earlier and gotten an eyeful of unframed canvases of angles, squares, and trapezoids in a showing of modern geometric art by an artist name Lynx. Yup. One of those one-name-only artistic types. A bunch of the frames had SOLD signs on them with a price tag of either $5,000 or $10,000. Too hard to tell from his quick visit if any of those canvases were the ones Eli had ferried out of the United States or, frankly, if said art would even be hanging on the wall at a gallery. But he wanted a local's opinion on the gallery, and no one was more local than a bartender. "Is that what I can get a few doors down?"

She whipped her head back and forth. "No way. You find that kind of stuff at cheap little tourist shops—" She clasped her hand on her mouth. Her brown eyes widened in embarrassment. "I'm sorry. I didn't mean for it to seem like I'm saying bad things about tourists."

Jake laughed and reassured her. "You're all good. You'll have to work pretty hard to offend me."

She wiped her hand across her brow. "Phew. I'm always just saying whatever comes to mind," she said, then dropped her voice to a whisper, since the bar was starting to fill up with other customers. "Not always the best trait for a bartender. Anyway, that gallery is more for fancier things."

Privately, he wondered precisely how fancy. Like $10 million fancy.

"Like my Renoir?" he asked drily.

She shot him a curious stare. "You better be joking. You don't really have a Renoir, do you?"

"Maybe I do. He was famous for his fishing scenes, right?"

Marie picked up the baton easily. "I believe the Louvre has some of those, don't they? Anyway, the gallery sells some fancy stuff, but nothing on that level. If you decide you want to turn that Renoir into diamonds instead, we've got plenty of shops for that, too."

"You've got a big diamond business on the Islands, right?"

"That we do. The great thing is when you buy one in the Caymans, it's tax-free. Business here is booming. All along the main street, and even the little shops on the side streets near the banks. Down on Wayboard Street—those guys have the best deals," she said, washing some glasses.

"So Wayboard Street is where I should go after I sell my Renoir to the lady next door?" he said with a wink.

"Absolutely," she said, pointing far off in the distance, as if to show him the street. "You pass this swank restaurant Tristan's, take a right, take your next right, and"—she stopped to issue a dramatic pause, fluttering her fingers like she was onstage—"and prepare to be dazzled."

He laughed and filed that data in the mental banks.

A group of new customers walked in, so Marie scurried to the tables, and Jake took out his phone and entered some notes. He finished his beer, tossed some bills on the bar, then some extra for Marie. That woman was a gold mine so far.

When he stood up to leave, he spotted a dartboard on the wall. Satisfied with his work so far today, he ambled over to it, picked up a few darts, then backed up several feet. Narrowing his eyes as if zeroing in on a target, he mimed tossing the dart once, twice, then a third time.

"You're shooting too high. You'll miss."

As he let the dart fly, his brain registered adjectives.

Sexy. Pretty. American.

He turned his head in the direction of the voice and . . . holy smokes. His assessment needed to be revised.

She was . . . beautiful.

Dark-blonde hair. Killer body. Legs a mile long and sculpted to toned perfection. Standing at the bar, knocking back a glass of whiskey. Totally at ease in her element.

He snapped his gaze to the dartboard. The dart was nowhere to be seen on the board. He'd missed by a mile, as predicted. The effect of a gorgeous woman. He turned his focus to her. "Seems I'm in need of a dart coach," he said, quirking up the corner of his lips, his acknowledgment that she'd bested him.

Setting her glass on the corner of the bar, she strolled past him and bent down.

Don't stare down her shirt. Stop gawking at that ass. Look away from the most perfect pair of legs you've ever seen.

As she plucked the dart from the ground, he tried to follow his own orders. He really tried. But he was failing on all accounts. Especially when her short little tank rode up and he caught sight of a sexy-as-sin belly button piercing.

Ah hell. That was just too tempting.

He drew a quick breath, as if that would settle the blast of lust threatening to camp out in his body right now. As she stood, she flashed him a bright smile, the kind that only an all-American girl could pull off. She looked that way, too—athletic, blue-eyed, and fresh-faced. Her hair was piled high on her head in some sort of ponytail contraption.

She handed him the dart. "I'll see if I have any openings in my schedule, Tommy," she said, roaming her eyes over his Tommy Bahama shirt. Another attempt to fit in. This shirt was so not his style.

He returned the favor, taking his time scanning her shirt with its smiling turtle illustration in the center. "Ah, so I was right. You're Happy Turtle, the dart coach, correct?" He tilted his head to the side in question, and she laughed lightly as he bestowed a shirt-derived name on her, too.

She lifted her chin. "If you hit a bull's-eye, I'll give you your first dart lesson free, Tommy."

"Can't back down from that kind of offer."

She leaned against the bar and took a drink as she eyed the board. She gestured to it, as if to say, *"Go ahead—impress me."*

Jake was no dart pro, but he'd spent enough time in bars and enough time with men killing time that he knew what he was doing. He'd only missed the first shot because of her. Now he'd need to land it because of her.

Instinct kicked in. The instinct that told a man to impress a pretty woman. Such a simple force, but a driving one for nearly any red-blooded male. He raised his arm, took aim, and let the dart fly. Straight down the middle. Landing the shot.

She cheered. Thrust her arms high above her head and hooted and hollered. "Admit it," she said, shaking a finger at him and narrowing her eyes. "You're a dart ringer. You've been sent by the National Federation of Dart Experts to infiltrate island bars and impress women with your dart skills."

"I've impressed you, then?" he asked, wanting to pump a fist and cheer at having accomplished his goal. Man, some days he was so damn simple. *See pretty woman; impress pretty woman.*

"You have indeed."

"Take your turn, then. Let's see how you do," he said, inviting her with a sweep of his arm.

She parked one hand on her hip. "You doubt me," she said with a curve of her lips. *Mmmm, those lips . . .* He shouldn't stare at them, either, but looking away from a pretty little mouth like that was cause for turning in your man card. He liked keeping his man card. And he liked entertaining images of those lips and how they'd taste and feel.

He shrugged as if to say, *"Bring it on."*

"Oh, you do! You totally doubt me. You think I marched in here, gave you orders, and can't back them up."

"Then show me, Happy Turtle," he said, ready to keep this flirty banter going on for however long it could last. As he egged her on, a realization smacked him hard—it had been a damn long time since he'd had this kind of a casual, random flirtation with a stranger. Maybe work and women didn't mix, but bars and beautiful women might be a perfect combination.

She took the dart from his hand slowly, making sure to brush her finger along his, or so it seemed. And hell, that slightest bit of contact tripped a switch in him. The switch that said more contact would be a fine way to spend the evening, thank you very much.

Matters south of the border started rising up.

Down, boy.

The woman never broke contact with his gaze as she stepped away. His brain didn't issue any orders to look elsewhere this time. She was inviting him to stare, and he did unabashedly, drinking her in, his analytical mind adding up details both practical and physical. The fact that she was here in a bar alone told him she was either an alcoholic or a local. The deep tan said local was more likely, and the bikini top, covered up by the tank and surf shorts, suggested she was a beach bum or simply part of the tourist industry. The toned legs and firm arms said she wasn't afraid to break a sweat.

He could think of plenty of ways to get sweaty with her.

She broke the eye contact, raised her arm, steadied her stance, and tossed. Right down the center.

"Holy shit," he said with a low whistle of appreciation.

She shrugged playfully and blew on her nails. *Too hot to handle.* "My stepdad taught me," she said, and something dark passed in those blue eyes when she said that, but it disappeared just as quickly as it came.

"He taught you well. But can you repeat?"

"Oh, ye of little faith," she said, taunting him as she jutted out her chin. She proceeded to demonstrate her dart prowess, landing shot after shot, and schooling him in the barroom game.

When the match ended and Jake was thoroughly demolished, he extended a hand. "Congratulations. You are officially a goddess of darts and I am humbly destroyed."

"I've always wanted to be a destructive goddess."

"By the way, real name's Jake."

"Mine's Ariel," she said.

He quirked his eyebrows together. "Like the mermaid?"

She nodded, her blue eyes lighting up. "Very good."

"Most men don't get the reference when you give them your fake bar name for strangers?"

Her eyes widened, nearly popping out of her head. Her mouth fell open. "Wait. You knew my name wasn't really Happy Turtle?"

He laughed, but he wasn't bothered by the fake name or the way she teased. "It's OK, *Ariel.* One, I have two sisters, so I know who Ariel is. Two, I have two sisters, so I know about fake bar names. Three, is your best friend a starfish?"

She leaned in closer, and he caught a faint whiff of her shampoo—smelled like coconuts. Perfect scent for an island woman. "I do that, too," she whispered.

"Do what?" he asked, furrowing his brow.

"That whole one, two, three thing."

"You count?" He pretended to sound shocked. He slapped a palm against the bar. "Then we absolutely, positively must meet up later for another drink," he said, and though the offer was made playfully, he fully meant it.

She shoved his shoulder. Oh, she was feisty. He liked that. "Listing numbers and answers—that's what I meant by the counting thing. And why do you ask if my best friend is a starfish?"

"One, you can do that again," he said, rubbing his shoulder. "I really enjoy getting smacked in the shoulder." She pretended to pout. "No, honestly. I do. It's this weird thing of mine. I completely crave shoulder punches," he said, in an intensely serious tone that made her curve up the corner of her lips and nudge his shoulder again, lightly this time. "Two, I knew what you meant by the counting thing. Three, I asked because I saw you have a starfish on your belly button, and it's ridiculously sexy."

CHAPTER FIVE

She'd had the piercing for years. So long she didn't even think about it anymore. She was barely aware of the sky-blue starfish belly ring that dangled along her stomach.

She ran her thumb across the sparkly surface. "I practically forgot I had this. Got it when I was sixteen."

"So a few years ago?"

"Ha ha ha," she said drily. "More than a few years."

"Well, you might have forgotten about it, but I could barely take my eyes off it," he said, his deep voice going low and sexy. Then he feigned seriousness. "I meant, while I was being a perfect gentleman and not checking out your smoking-hot body when you bent down to pick up the dart—that's when I noticed the starfish."

She tingled all over from the compliment. There was something so enticing about this kind of praise from this kind of man. He was tall, built, strong, and with the kind of jawline that made a woman want to reach out and touch that face. That made *this woman* want to run her thumb along his sandpaper stubble, feel it brush against her chin, and mouth, and lips.

His brown hair boasted golden streaks, and his green eyes crinkled at the corners. Something about the whole package, sans the Tommy Bahama shirt, said *strong and rugged*. Which was an utterly delicious combination, one that made her skin warm up all over and her mind wander just a little further into *let's-picture-him-undressed* land. Yup, she could see him clearly in her mind's eye: hard planes across his chest, grooves in firm abs, arms so strong she couldn't even wrap a hand around them.

She blinked, like she was a computer rebooting, as she tried to chase away the dirty thoughts landing in her head. But that body. Oh Lord, that body could cause some kind of sin.

His body should come with a warning. *Gaze upon said hotness and arousal will be yours.*

She needed to focus on why she was here on this island. Recon. Information. Getting the lay of the land before she connected with her stepdad. The thought that she'd find out he'd screwed over her mom in an even worse way made her shoulders tighten. Only the hope that she'd uncover something else, that it wasn't what it seemed, could help them ease. She'd stopped in the Pink Pelican on a hunt for a sweet but flighty gal named Penny, who had tended bar last time Steph was here. Penny preferred to spend her days kiteboarding and rock climbing. Penny's sister Marie was manning the taps now, and Steph hadn't even had a chance to say a proper hello.

"Well, thank you for saying that."

"My pleasure. And it is also a pleasure to meet you, Ariel," he said, extending a hand to shake.

Don't think about pulling him against you. Stop imagining what his body would feel like above you. No more staring at those full lips and wondering how they taste, and feel, and . . .

Fuck it.

This man was hot and fun, and that was a mixture she liked *a lot*. After the extreme focus she'd placed on rehabbing her business in the last few years, a little bit of sexy flirting was a welcome relief. Maybe her mom was right. Maybe Steph did need to have a little fun.

"Is it really Jake?" she said, not letting go of his hand, enjoying the way his name sounded. "Or did you pick a fake name, too? Because Jake is the perfect name for a totally hot guy a woman meets in a bar."

He smiled widely, and she loved that it seemed to light up his whole face, all the way to his green eyes. He was handsome and then some, but the reaction, so genuine, was lovely to see. So rare to compliment a man and to witness the evidence of his enjoyment of it. "Yes, the name is really Jake, and thank you. Seems we have a mutual admiration society at work here."

"Yes," she said with a small grin. "There is much admiration, and I'm glad it's mutual." As she let go of his grip, her eyes drifted to a white, raised mark on his forearm. "By the way, cool scar. Is it a new acquisition?"

He tapped his forearm. "Yes it is. Wish I could say the acquisition was intentional."

"It wasn't?"

He shook his head.

"What happened?" She flung her hand to her forehead, like a fortune-teller reading the cards. "Wait. Don't tell me. You got in a knife fight in an alley, Jason Bourne style? You've gone rogue and the CIA is after you? Or better yet, you slipped while gutting a fish after one too many beers?"

He pointed at her. "That one."

She mimed tossing a basketball. "She shoots. She scores." She tilted her head. "But seriously?"

"What can I say? Fishing and beer go together, but not when knives are involved."

She wagged a finger at him. "You gotta be careful there, Jake."

"I know, I know. Maybe if I catch anything tomorrow, I could find a mermaid to help me."

"Mermaids don't like it when you catch fish. Or turtles."

"That is true. Pretend I never said that. I would never catch a fish. I'm absolutely not here on a fishing trip. In fact, I'm here to admire the gorgeous scenery."

She nodded approvingly. "Much better answer."

He pointed to her glass, nearly empty. "Can I get you another whiskey?"

"It's iced tea, actually, and I'm trying to cut back, so I'm all good."

"Been hitting the caffeine too hard?"

She nodded solemnly. "Evidently, when I drink too much, it makes me say things I shouldn't say. Like *totally hot guy* in a bar."

He grinned and held up the glass as if to ask for more. "Let's make it a double," he said, and after they chatted more about fish and the sea and the Islands, he pointed to the dartboard. "Since you have that dart certification and all, any chance you can give me a few pointers?" he asked, standing up to grab a dart from the board. He returned and held it out to her. She rose and moved closer, and when she reached for the end, he wrapped a hand around her wrist and tugged her in close.

Just like that. The gauntlet was thrown. The move was made. She was in his arms. *Poised.* For something more. For this moment to unspool into something else. A ribbon of heat raced through her body as she catalogued everything. His gaze held her hostage. His green eyes blazed darkly as he stared at her like he wanted to eat her up. That fierce look made her shudder. She was so close she could breathe him in, and his skin smelled so damn good. Like sunshine and showers. And he was hard everywhere. Not just *there*, because she wasn't exactly in that spot, but his arms, and his abs, and his legs.

His fingers curled around her waist, gripping her as Jack Johnson sang about banana pancakes and pretending it's the weekend all the time.

"Three things," he whispered, his voice all rough and hot, turning her on before he even uttered another word. "One, I want to kiss you.

Two, I'm going to kiss you. Three, if you don't want me to, say no now. Otherwise . . ."

He inched closer. She parted her lips, and a small sigh escaped. "Yes."

She closed her eyes and waited. In that second before his lips met hers, the wondrous thrill of anticipation weaved through her body. The hope that kissing a stranger named Jake in a bar would be worth it. That he wouldn't kiss like a slobbery Saint Bernard, all tongue and exuberance. Nor like a schoolboy, hell-bent on vacuuming up her lips. Call her greedy, call her needy, or just call her a woman who hadn't been kissed well in a long while.

But she wanted *that* kiss.

The kind that made your knees weak.

That sent your heart fluttering.

That spread warmth on a sweet, shivery path through your chest.

His lips met hers. His were so damn soft, and full, and delicious. He didn't rush it. He took his time, exploring her mouth, brushing his lips over hers, tasting her. That tingly sensation sped up, shooting through her, like an injection of pure, unadulterated pleasure as she melted into his kiss.

He was snug against her, and she savored it—the delicious press of his body as he swept his lips across hers, his touch making her moan. The kiss deepened as he ran his fingertips along her bare arm, igniting her skin. He dropped his hand to her lower back, angling her closer, and oh, how she'd craved this kind of closeness. Badly. She wanted to climb him. She wanted to feel him above her, moving in her, holding her tight. This rampant desire was a matchstick. Roping her arms around his neck, she curled her fingers into the ends of his hair.

Oh, that soft hair. God, it felt good between her fingers as she slid them through his golden brown strands, tugging lightly.

He groaned and yanked her even closer. The quick shift in tempo moved the kiss up the heat ladder into something hungrier. He held her face in his hands, a thoroughly possessive gesture, as he kissed her so hard his stubble left a whiskery burn.

The evidence of a consuming kiss.

Her mind spun wild with images. Pictures of this night turning into something else. Kisses under the stars. Hips, legs, lips moving together. Him wrapping her tighter in his caress, whispering sweet, dirty things he wanted to do to her. In the heat of his kiss, in the urgency of his touch, she had the raw materials to feed her imagination.

Her heart raced. Her blood pumped. She craved him fiercely.

Which was absolutely loony, since he was a total stranger.

But maybe that's what fueled her desire. They had no history. They had no past. There was no damage or pain between them. He hadn't hurt her, he hadn't lied to her, and he hadn't tried to fling her business into the trash. No, he had one agenda, it seemed. The same one she had.

Let's spend the night together.

He backed her up against the wall, next to the dartboard, her spine hitting the wood with a thump. The sound of it was like a door shutting. Like the moment when a kiss turns from *we're trying this on for size* to *this kiss won't stop at kissing*. He cupped the back of her neck, and his other hand clasped her hip, yanking her against him, so she could feel *him*.

She could feel *all of him*.

Lust skyrocketed in her, on a mad dash to cloud her reason, her judgment, to ambush all remaining sanity. To simply crush the logical, thoughtful portions of her brain. Lock them up and throw away the key, so she could go somewhere, anywhere, with Jake and let him—

His phone rang.

A Taylor Swift song.

Instantly, he broke the kiss and sighed deeply, a frustrated sound.

"One of your fishing buddies rescuing you from the woman in a bar who won't give her name?" Steph asked, catching her breath as she arched an eyebrow.

He shook his head and scrubbed his hand over his jaw. "My little sister. That's her ringtone." He swiped his thumb across the phone. "Kylie, give me five seconds," he said into the phone, then covered the screen. He quickly scanned the bar, on the hunt for something. Steph wasn't sure what he wanted, and she was still punch-drunk on that kiss, so her brain wasn't fully processing. He shot out his arm, grabbed a napkin, and handed it to her.

"Give me a number. So I can call you later," he said.

Did she want to give him her number?

A sob sounded from the phone. Her heart raced with worry. She hoped his sister was OK. She pointed in the general direction of the bar. "I'll leave it with Marie. I have somewhere I need to be now anyway. But you can reach me later, I guess," she said, the words coming out in a stumble, like a car sputtering to turn on. Her brain clearly needed a few seconds, maybe even minutes, to string language together again.

"I'll be back," he said, then he walked out in a rush.

Steph let out a breath and stared at the empty space where he'd been, then she replayed the last few minutes and knit her brow.

On the one hand, he'd asked for her number.

But on the other hand, he was . . . gone.

Little sister? Was that the new excuse? The escape hatch to jettison a man from a bad date? She had no clue because she'd been out of commission for a couple years. Was that what guys said when they didn't like the way a woman kissed? What if *little sister* was an eject button or something? Absently, she raised her fingers to her lips. They still tingled. She ran the pad of a finger over her bottom lip.

"Steph!"

She swiveled around, spotting Marie behind the bar. She had been waiting on tables when Steph first walked in. "It's been too long," Marie said, then flashed her a naughty look. "But I see you've already gotten to know Jake the Fisherman. Looks like you two were going to gobble each other up."

A huge grin spread across her face. That was all she needed. Nothing wrong with her lips. That kiss had blown her mind, and likely his, too. Mutual gobbling and all.

She wasn't going to let self-doubt rule the day. Nope.

"Do me a favor, Marie?" she asked as she snagged a pen from the register and wrote a few words on the napkin. No number for him just yet. If Jake wanted to see her, he was going to have to follow her trail.

"Of course."

"Actually, two favors. Tell Penny I can't wait to see her."

Marie nodded. "She's camping. Should be back in a few days."

"She'd better call me while I'm here. Then give this to the hot fisherman if he comes back in here. But don't tell him my name, OK?"

Marie rubbed her hands together and winked. "Ooh, lover games. And I get to be the messenger. Count me in."

Steph handed Marie the note, then took off for her first stop on her self-appointed job.

CHAPTER SIX

Pacing along the street with his cell phone pressed to his ear, Jake used his best big-brother voice to try to calm Kylie. "Everything is going to be fine. We'll figure it out, I promise."

Kylie gulped, like she was hyperventilating. "I don't know what to do. I barely understand a word the physics professor says. It's like he's speaking a foreign language. I don't know how on earth I'm going to finish school without this science requirement. I suck at science. I can't do this, Jake. I can't do this at all."

"You're going to do fine. If you don't understand the subject matter, we'll get you a tutor," he said as he walked past a surf shop with signs in the window for adventure tours.

"But what if it doesn't help?" His little sister's voice shot high up into the sky. Kylie, to put it lightly, was prone to worrying. She'd always been the nervous one among the bunch, and that intensified when they lost their parents. The baby of the family, she was seven when the four of them were orphaned and went to live with an older aunt who managed a restaurant in Key Largo. Truth be told, Kate and then Jake had done most of the parenting. Despite their best efforts, Kylie had grown up a world-class worrier, and that anxiety had manifested in her schoolwork all through high school and now into college. The best way to help her through it was to give her very clear instructions. That also meant phone calls with Kylie required lots of time and patience, which was why he'd had to extract himself from the bar so he could focus on his family. They came first and always would.

The aftereffects of Ariel still lingered, though, because that had been one hot, intense kiss that was on the cusp of rocketing quickly into so much more. A tremor of lust started to roll through him with the memory, so he squeezed his eyes shut, forcing his damn brain to focus on family matters, not primal ones.

He was here for work, not *personal* needs. Even on a job, he still needed to look out for his little sister. Take care of her, help her. Guide her step by step.

"You're catastrophizing, Kylie. You need to stop assuming it won't work before we even hire one. We've talked about this before. You can't get worked up over what hasn't happened. Got it?"

"I know, I know," she muttered.

"Now listen," he said, turning down the block. "I need you to ask around at your school. Get some names. Share them with me. I'll talk to them, and we'll find the right tutor for you."

"I'm such a fuck up," she said, another sob threatening to rear its head. "You probably never struggled in school."

"You're not a fuck up," he said gently, but in a voice that brooked no argument. "Stop beating yourself up. You just need some help. That's all. Nothing wrong with that. Do some research, get me the info, and I will take care of it. I promise you."

"But tutors are so expensive."

"Kylie," he said, stopping in his tracks, slicing a hand through the air. He didn't want her to spiral like this. He needed to yank her out of this with some tough love. "What have I told you before?"

She sighed. "Not to worry about money."

"Exactly. So stop it right now. No more of this. No more talk of being a fuck up, and no more stressing about money. Your job is to focus on school. My job is to focus on taking care of the school bills. Just let me do that," he said, and after she took a few calming breaths, she asked him about his work and the weather in the Caribbean.

"It's beautiful here."

"What were you doing when I called? Did I interrupt a tanning session on the beach?"

He laughed. "Just talking to someone I met playing darts."

"A girl?"

"None of your business," he said playfully.

"That definitely means you met a girl, then," she said, teasing him like she was a schoolkid. He let her, not denying it this time, because it seemed to take her mind off her school anxiety.

After she finished a thorough ribbing, he told her he loved her and said good-bye.

He glanced up at the sky. The sun had started to dip toward the horizon, pulling streaks of orange and pink like a tail. He checked out the time.

Fifteen minutes had passed.

Maybe Ariel was still at the bar.

Maybe fish could fly.

But a man could hope, and a man could pick up the pace just in case. Jake turned up his speedometer and jogged past a jewelry shop selling seashell necklaces and silvery trinkets, then a store full of sundresses, then one with the sign for tours in the window. He nearly did a double take when he spotted a poster with a familiar name for a cove on the beach.

He filed the name away in the mental banks.

When he returned to the Pink Pelican, he scanned left, then right, then up and down. The woman he'd wanted to take home for the night was nowhere to be found.

His shoulders sagged, and he cursed himself for not having grabbed the number before he left.

But he just might have one more shot. Because the world's most helpful bartender was calling him over. Marie's eyes lit up with excitement. He recognized that look. His sister Kate had it from time to time when she tried to wear her matchmaker hat.

Marie waved the napkin in the air, brandishing it like a prize. "A pretty lady gave me this for you."

Straightening his spine, he unfolded it, then chuckled when he saw what she had done. No number. Just a clue. He liked clues. Oh hell, did he like clues.

Especially this one.

∽

The pictures at the snorkel shop taunted her.

They told the story of the luckiest man she'd ever known. On top of the frames, the proprietor of the shop had stenciled a mantra in blue paint on the wall: KISS A RAY AND GET SEVEN YEARS OF LUCK.

In a trio of images, her stepfather's magnetic smile shone through. In the first shot, a young, blond, and tanned Eli Thompson pressed his lips to the smooth, silvery skin of a stingray. Steph hadn't partaken of the kiss fest, because she was only seven at the time and kissing any sort of creature, underwater or above water, was certifiably gross. But in the background of the photo, she laughed at her stepdad, sharing the same sense of adventure that the man had possessed. Growing up, she'd considered him her hero. He'd been the man who made her mom happy again.

Her mother had been devastated when her husband—Steph and Robert's father—had died so unexpectedly. Widowed at a young age, with two toddlers, her mom didn't have the easiest time of it. But she made do and soldiered on, and a few years later she met Eli.

The man had made her mom laugh again. Made her feel happiness. He was like that. Delight seemed to be his native language. Now it made Steph's chest twinge to think it was all part of his routine—cover up his straying ways with his sunshine smile.

In the next stingray lip-lock photo, his hair was a touch thinner and a bit darker, but his light blue eyes had that same confident spark. Steph had inched close enough to blow a kiss to the stingray in that one. "You'll kiss him next time," Eli had said to her.

The final picture was taken during a family vacation—she'd joined Eli and her mom here after her junior year of college. On that visit, Steph had gone all in and puckered up to the stingray for the first time. But she'd missed right when her lips would have landed on its skin.

The ray had slipped away. Taking her luck with it, too.

She moved closer to the photo and quirked up the corner of her lips as she peered at the image she hadn't seen in years, flashing back to all their trips here. Eli had taken them here nearly every year. This island became a second home for her new family growing up, and her stepdad had glad-handed with all the locals. He'd been the man about town. Like an ambassador who everyone loved and was delighted to see when he descended on the island. He'd brought good fortune to them, they said.

Always tipping well, always partaking of all the local customs, always embracing the legends.

Maybe her stepdad was right to believe in this legend. Perhaps she should have kissed a stingray sooner or held on longer for the last one. She should have insisted on her luck, the way Eli seemed predestined to claim his.

Breezing through life, flashing a grin, taking what he wanted because he could. Because he had that thing known as charm.

Duke had that, too. She'd fallen for him because he had an easy way about him. The second things didn't go his way he'd turned into a complete asshole.

She winced, hoping, praying, that Eli wasn't all bad. Not like Duke. That's why she was here in the Islands early. To find out which side of her stepfather was the true one.

She drummed her fingers against the counter, waiting for Devon to finish up with his customer. She'd known Devon since she was that towheaded seven-year-old, and he'd been running this snorkel shop next to Stingray City Sandbar for even longer. His rough, dark skin told the tale of his years as a sun worshipper, and the steady stream of traffic in his store showed that he'd made a damn good living renting gear and operating boat tours for visitors to mingle in the crystal-blue waters with the world's friendliest stingrays.

"But don't they, you know, sting you?" a woman with big sunglasses and gold hoop earrings asked him in a Jersey accent.

He waved a hand to reassure her, then mimed petting a dog. "Nah. They're like little puppies. They know you have food, so they get all excited and cuddle up next to you."

"I do like puppies," the woman said, standing taller.

"'Course you do. Now, go enjoy the puppies of the water," he said in his cheery voice.

The customer thanked him, then headed out to join the rest of the tour group.

Devon held his arms out wide and flashed a huge grin at Steph, his white teeth gleaming. "Give me a hug. It has been far too long," he said as she embraced him. He stepped away as if taking her in, like a family friend who hadn't seen her in a long time. Of course, in many ways, that's what he was. But he was also *her* friend and had been since she'd started up her business. He'd stood by her even when times had been tough. He'd always put in a good word for her when he could, and she'd done the same for him.

Guys like him almost erased the memory of guys like Duke.

"I know. I miss you all," she said softly, since losing her traction here had hurt her heart the most.

"Then get your butt down here more often," he said, pointing wildly to the floor, the ceiling, the window that offered the most gorgeous view of endless blue water and sky.

"I'm doing my best. I've got a tour next week, and you know I'll be bringing them here to your shop," she said with a wide smile, grateful to chat about work for the moment. Getting to the heart of her visit would be tougher—intel about Eli.

"Hey! Can we do that thing we used to do? Where we plant a little treasure chest on the sandbar?"

Steph cracked up, clasping her belly at the memory of their antics. On a few of their guided stingray city tours, they'd actually lugged a wooden chest into the water and lined it with huge, and clearly fake, gems. Visitors had gotten a kick out of the notion of discovering a pirate's booty. Funny thing was, despite all the tales and stories of buried treasure and pirates, in reality there weren't many documented findings of treasure maps or undersea discoveries throughout history.

Only fiction. Only lore.

"We have to do that again. That was our greatest hit."

He scratched his chin. "Hey, I have a private group at the end of the week. A short couples-only visit to the stingrays. Want to help out?"

She nodded enthusiastically. "I would love to. Text me the details?"

"Absolutely." He tipped his forehead to her in question. "So you came to town early? Any special reason?" He fixed her with a stare that said he was waiting.

Nerves skated across her skin. She took a breath and segued into the real reason for her stop. *Recon.* This was odd for her, since she'd never needed her local friends for information before. But now she did, and she'd have to ask in a way that didn't reveal her true motives—to find out what her stepdad was up to and whether any of his actions suggested he'd been up to no good with other people's money.

Sure, she planned to call him later and make plans to see him. But she needed to be smart and gather some info first. It wasn't like she could just show up at Eli's house asking about his finances. Even inquiring about how business was going would raise a red flag, since they'd never had those conversations in the past. He was far too shrewd to fall for that sort of questioning. That's why she was going in through the side door, tucking away potentially useful details before she saw him.

"So, Devon," she said, clearing her throat. "I need your honest opinion on something."

"Uh-oh."

"It's not bad."

He arched an eyebrow. "It's never good when someone says they want an honest opinion."

Devon was Switzerland. He had nothing against her stepdad. Eli had been a reliable customer for years, so she had to be careful, to tread a fine line. "I want your unbiased opinion. Now that business is picking up for me again, I need to do everything to run a tight ship and make sure customers are happy. So when someone on a tour asks me about the nightlife . . . ," she said, then made a rolling gesture with her hand.

Devon's mouth formed an *O* and he nodded like a wise man. "I get it. You want to know how Sapphire is doing."

She mimed whacking a hammer. "As always, you hit the nail on the head."

"That place is red-hot. All the young people are partying hard there. They talk it up when they come in the next day. It's a huge hit. Crowds every night. Packed to the gills. It's like a goddamn mint."

Mint.

She gritted her teeth, biting back the comments that threatened to fall from her lips. *Is Eli making a mint with someone else's money? Did his company unknowingly fund that damn club?* She sucked down those words, because this was what she needed to know. Eli Thompson still had the Midas touch. Nothing changed.

She leaned across the counter and planted a soft kiss on Devon's leathery cheek. He pretended to catch the kiss in his hand. "Now I've got my next seven years."

"If only a kiss from me had such powers."

"Oh, I suspect it has great powers."

She returned to a kiss from a few hours ago and sent a silent wish to the universe that Jake had come back for her note, that he'd decipher it, and that she'd see him again. So bizarre to want to see a stranger so badly. But perhaps kisses did have great powers. His had the power to make her long for him. The man whose last name she didn't even know.

Devon parked his hands on her shoulders. "Hey, I know your parents split up, and it wasn't so pretty the way it all went down. I get that you're not on the greatest terms with your stepdad, and that's a damn shame," he said, and though Devon wasn't privy to every sordid detail, he knew enough about how hard the divorce had been from her conversations with him during her visits. "But I'm all for family getting along and putting the past behind them, and I hope you're able to do that. Even though he's not your flesh and blood, he's the man I saw taking care of you when you were a kid," he said, and she pursed her lips, wishing what he'd said wasn't true. Because it would be so much easier to write Eli off as an asshole if it were.

"Just remember—he's done some real good here," Devon added. "He hired a bunch of local companies when he built out his club. He did his part to invest in the Cayman economy, and a lot of folks here have been damn grateful for the business he's brought to them. He did right by a lot of people when he remodeled the club. Penny even did some work for him before she started working at a flower shop. Assistant type stuff when he was setting it up last year. He was real good to her, I hear."

"Penny?" Steph asked, as if the name of the woman she knew was suddenly foreign. She couldn't picture pink-haired, tattooed Penny working for her stepdad, but this little nugget was all the more reason to track down her friend. Penny was a free spirit, a true island girl who flitted from random job to random job, sometimes as a nanny, sometimes as a Girl Friday, sometimes as a dog walker.

Penny had just moved near the top of the list of people to see. Someone else was on that list, too.

Later that night in her small and exceedingly cheap hotel room, she called the man of the hour, bracing herself to hear that voice she'd so adored as a kid. The happy, carefree sound of the man who had helped raise her.

"Sweetheart!"

His voice boomed loudly above the sound of music. The music faded, and the background noise died. He must have moved someplace quieter.

"Hey there, Eli," she said. "I'm in town. Want to have brunch tomorrow?"

CHAPTER SEVEN

Drum-heavy techno music pulsed loudly.

Actually, *vibrated* was a more accurate way to describe the volume. The electronic beat of the music reverberated in his bones as Jake weaved through the sardine-packed crowds thronging the dance floor.

The nightclub lived up to its name.

The sleek, silvery Sapphire shimmered. Mirrored walls behind the bar were edged with neon blue. Jewel-toned lights flashed from the ceiling, moving and swaying in colored spotlights. Women in barely there black dresses that skimmed the top of their thighs on one end and plumped up their chests on the other sidled up beside girlfriends or next to men. The crowd was mostly young, but sprinkled with the evidence of tourists of many ages—the mom and dad on a getaway from the kids, groups of fortysomething friends reliving their younger days with a hot night on the town, and lots of single men, from frat boys up to sugar-daddy age.

Jake leaned against the bar, soaking it in, taking mental notes about Eli's new world. Everything sparkled. The lights, the bar, and the disco ball. His eyes roamed the dance floor, then he raised them higher, up to the second level, and he saw him.

No question about it.

That man had to be Eli Thompson. The face matched the images Jake had scoped out online. Like a middle-age Robert Redford, Eli had that golden-boy look to him still. He rested his hands on the railing and surveyed the scene, like a prince presiding over his subjects.

Jake narrowed his eyes. What a sneaky fucker. Stealing from his company, skipping out of town with it in art. Maybe even turning that art back into dough here in the Caribbean.

Funny thing, though. If Eli had poured the dollars he pilfered into this club, the man had picked wisely—much better than his failed cocoa bean investment. But it sounded like the cocoa beans were meant to fail. So he could have this, perhaps? Jake scratched his chin, wondering if this club was the endgame—did the man steal to build this new business?

Judging from the liquor flowing, the cover charge, and the lack of elbow room, the man was making money hand over fist, and he played the part well with a crisp button-down and tailored pants. A feline-esque woman with jet-black hair and a wine-red dress joined him, wrapping an arm around his waist. Eli glanced briefly at her, clasping her hand, then stopping to run a finger across the hollow of her throat.

The new woman in his life. Something about her throat interested Eli. Which meant it interested Jake.

Setting his glass of ice water on the bar, he worked his way to the coiled metal staircase at the edge of the dance floor. Keeping his eyes on Eli and the woman, he headed up the steps as quickly as he could, given the heavy press of crowds pushing in both directions. His focus narrowed to the two of them. Like a sniper staring down the barrel of a gun, he only saw Eli and his lady. He rounded the corner as the woman planted a kiss on Eli's cheek.

Eli cupped her face in his hand and returned the smooch, his fingers drifting to her neckline. Even from Jake's spot ten feet away, he was nearly blinded. The stone on her necklace was brighter than the sun, and it was the object of Eli's affection. Stroking it, caressing it, fondling the stone, the man was fixated on her rock. Jake managed to sneak a few feet closer to snag a better look at the stone. Square, with just a trace of a bluish tint to it.

Like a sapphire.

Eli was dating an art dealer, all right, but the man sure seemed fonder of jewels than art. And there *was a big diamond business on the Islands.*

Before they could see him, he swiveled around. As he walked to the exit, Jake played connect the dots in his head. Money, art, diamonds, club. He didn't have enough information yet to draw a conclusion, but he didn't want to leave any stones unturned. He peered up at the balcony one more time—Eli reached into his pocket and pressed his cell phone to his ear. In two seconds, his face lit up with an almost child-like glee. Whoever had called him had made the man's day. Eli turned around and opened a door, extracting himself from the crowds.

Jake reached the exit, too, where a burly security guard manned the door. His arms were crossed, revealing ink on his forearm of his rank in the army. Jake had put himself through college thanks to the army ROTC, then traveled to Europe where he was stationed with the 66th Military Intelligence Brigade.

"Staff Sergeant," Jake said to the man with a nod, reading his stripes.

The big man raised his gaze, and the expression in his eyes shifted from one of standoffishness to connection. "Yes."

Jake tapped his chest. "Captain. Six years."

"Served for seven myself," he said, then named his unit. "Cal Winters."

"Jake Harlowe."

"Thank you for your service."

"Thank you for your service."

A while later, at his hotel, he researched his plan of attack for tomorrow, and also tackled Kylie's tutor project, firing off e-mails to a few of the names she'd sent him already. Then, as he lay in bed, he unfolded the napkin from the Pink Pelican and tapped his fingertips against his chin as he reread the details. Earlier, he'd been certain he'd follow this trail back to Ariel. But, through no fault of the woman, tonight's visit to Sapphire had reminded him that this was no easy job. He'd only just begun, and he had a lot of legwork ahead of him to get to the bottom of the missing $10 million. Finding stolen goods wasn't for the faint of heart.

Hell, the best gigs with the biggest payoffs were the toughest ones, with the most twists and turns on the road.

Distractions like beautiful women were ultimately just that—distractions. They were pitfalls that could rattle his concentration on an assignment that didn't yet have a direct path to the prize.

But was there room for a little tryst on the side? He'd never liked to mix business with pleasure. Ever since the romance with Rosalinda went belly-up, he'd been a rules man through and through, and the number-one rule was to maintain lines. Rosalinda's trickery had endangered the assignment and nearly cost him one of the biggest jobs he'd ever nabbed—the payoff for the Medici gig had gone a long way in funding Kylie's college bills.

Thank Christ he'd caught up with Rosalinda in that damn shoe store.

He pressed his thumb and forefinger against the bridge of his nose, crumpling the napkin with his other hand, balling it up.

Best to forget Ariel. Do the job. Get in. Get out. Get home.

But then, as he tossed the napkin in the trash can near the door, he rewound to those moments in the Pink Pelican. Images played before him of her delicious lips, the swell of her breasts, her sexy-as-sin legs, and most of all—the way she fit in his arms. That kiss had obliterated his brain cells, and now the rich, ripe memory of it was making it hard to think about anything else.

Too hard.

Try as he might to banish all thoughts of her, he couldn't get her out of his mind. Nor could he erase the effects on his body just from thinking of her.

He rose, walked over to the trash can, and fished for the piece of paper. He read it one more time. It said:

123. Happy Turtle. Tomorrow.

Fuck it.

He was an adult. He could handle this. He could see her again and still do his job. Besides, nothing more was going to come of a little rendezvous. This would merely be a lush tropical affair. She had nothing whatsoever to do with the job. He was fine. Completely fine and maintaining those all-important lines.

He'd keep things separate from work and enjoy a little something with quite possibly the sexiest woman he'd ever met.

CHAPTER EIGHT

The next morning, Jake waited in his rental car a safe distance outside Eli's house, keen to gather some intel on the man's habits. Sunglasses on and ball cap pulled low, he roamed his gaze over the house. The silhouette of a tall man wandered past a window on the second floor a few times. Jake couldn't make out what room the window opened into. Bedroom maybe. Perhaps an office. Or even a hallway.

Peering through mini binoculars, he tried to scope out the scene. No luck. Too many branches from trees framed the home, and blinds covered most of the windows.

He lowered the binoculars and kept his eyes on the front door. As he waited, he alternated between watching the house and answering e-mails from potential tutors for Kylie. His sister had also texted him this morning—an emoticon of lips smooching.

He sent her back a monkey, covering his mouth. He was glad that her playful side was still alive and well, despite her overarching worries about school.

Then, he thumbed through Kate's e-mails about inquiries from new clients.

> Have I told you before you need to bring
> someone else on board? Lots of work coming
> our way.

He sure did enjoy those words *lots of work*, because lots of work was the one guaranteed way for him to pay off all the college bills for his brothers and sisters.

> Excellent. Try Dan if it's not too crazy a job.

Dan was a buddy from Jake's army days who picked up occasional work with his firm. Dan could certainly handle the so-called crazy jobs, but Jake still preferred to take those on himself. Like this one. There was so much that was open-ended about this job and so many potential directions. He thrived on hunting down the leads, circling the evidence, and then nailing the goods.

Nailing.

Wrong word, because it whipped him right back to last night and exactly what he'd been picturing when he was alone in his hotel room. His brain had been working those images hard before he fell asleep. He was damn eager to see his dart coach again today, but he shoved all thoughts of that hot blonde from his mind when Eli strolled down the stone path of his house, tossing his keys lightly in one hand. Eli stopped to admire an orchid tree, then bent his head toward a bush of red roses, wafting the scent toward his nostrils with his other hand. The man really did know how to enjoy himself. From the nightclub to his lush tropical home, Eli Thompson seemed to savor every little moment that his life laid out before him on a red carpet.

Eli raised his face to the sky and held his arms out to the side. Like he was inviting the glory of the sun into his day. Jake laughed to himself. What must it be like to stroll through the day with that kind of devil-may-care attitude? That attitude must be precisely what allowed Eli to take money that wasn't his. Jake clenched his jaw. The reminder of Eli's thievery fueled him.

The man walked to his car in the driveway—a gleaming black Audi.

Minutes later, Jake drove a few vehicles behind him as Eli motored toward town. "Thank you very much, Mr. Thompson. That's exactly where I'm headed after I follow you," Jake said to himself.

He slowed at a red light, a few cars behind Eli, and alongside a green Honda. The light changed, and Eli jetted into the financial district.

Banks, banks, and more banks lined the main street that cut through the heart of Grand Cayman, slicing the island into water and money.

To Jake's left, the ocean stretched as far as the eye could see, a vast sheet of cool blue. To his right, row after row of big, imposing white structures towered high, with names like Royal Bank and Cayman Finance that promised to squirrel away your coins for as long as you needed them abracadabra-ed.

No questions asked. No explanations needed. Just open the account, drop in some dough, and your money gets all the insulation it could ever need. Sleek black cars rolled along the concrete stretch of street, dropping off sharp-dressed women in monochrome skirts and blouses and men in crisp suits and ties, their outfits a stark contrast to the island lifestyle. The bankers had their own uniform—that of the financiers who had made this country wealthy, and made shady businessmen and women richer.

The man in question parked outside a tall, stark white bank.

Jake grabbed a nearby spot and was about to venture into the same bank, when Eli popped back out. Whoa. That was fast. Eli couldn't have been in the bank long enough to do anything but grab a few bucks at the ATM. No chance he'd dropped off any hefty sums of cash or checked on goods in a safe deposit box.

Jake ducked out of the way of the revolving door, then walked purposefully to the gurgling fountain with an angel statue outside the bank. He fished for some coins in his pocket and tossed them in, making a wish that this job would pay off.

Eli crossed the street, then headed up a set of steps to a chichi restaurant called Tristan's with a terrace one story up from the road. Eli rapped on the door, and a tall man answered it, letting him in. Jake couldn't get a good look at the guy; he only saw a head full of salt-and-pepper hair. Once Eli was inside, Jake walked up the steps.

The restaurant was quiet and the sign said OPEN FOR BRUNCH AT TEN.

He glanced at his watch. That was one hour from now. *What was Eli doing here so early?* He must be meeting with someone who worked there, and Jake would add Tristan's to the list of places to check out. For now, this extra hour gave him time to get some other work done. After he left, he weaved through the late-morning crowds in the financial district, until he turned on a side street that boasted smaller banks, perhaps for smaller deposits. He cruised by a few offices, until he reached Wayboard Street with small storefronts bearing signs like DUTY-FREE, WHOLESALE, and UNCUT.

The last one sounded vaguely like a porno flick. He shuddered at the thought, and then shoved it out of his brain.

Rolling the dice, because that was all he could do, he tried the first diamond shop.

Given Eli's laser focus on that rock on his fiancée's throat, as well as Marie's comment about gems, Jake wanted to take the temperature of the diamond business.

Posing as a curious customer, he spoke briefly with the proprietor, but the man was deluged with new customers and quickly told him he didn't have and hadn't seen any diamonds with a bluish tint.

Undeterred, he tried another shop. A pear-shaped man with a metal nose ring—such an odd accessory for a guy peddling jewels—tried to pitch him on walking out the door *right this very second* with a 20 percent discount on a fair-trade diamond set in a white gold band that was a size six but could be reset for the woman of Jake's dreams.

No such woman fit the bill.

At the next shop, Jake used the weather as a warm-up, with a simple remark about the sunshine.

"They say not every day in the Caymans is wonderful," the woman replied. "For instance, we only get sunshine and perfect temperatures three hundred and sixty-four days of the year."

"That three hundred and sixty-fifth day is a rough one, isn't it," Jake replied with a smile as he perused the jewels. "I trust business is as fantastic as the weather?"

He was met with a blank stare. Then a curt "yes."

She bent down to straighten out some displays, making it clear to Jake she wasn't the type to gab about who was moving what in carats these days.

"Thanks for your time," he said on the way out, peering down the block, hunting for more. He was flying blind on this recon mission. There were no guarantees he'd glean anything useful from this trip, but he had to keep trying. Porny name or not, he headed into Uncut at the end of the block. The glass cases by the wall were lined with so many necklaces, they nearly blinded him.

A dark-haired man with a thick beard and an eager grin strode up to him. "Greetings and welcome to Uncut, where we specialize in the best duty-free diamonds on the island," the man said, sounding like a TV commercial. "Are you looking for something for that special someone?"

"Potentially."

The man placed his hands together, as if in prayer. "Ah, excellent. So this is for a lovely woman in your life you want to make your wife?"

Jake laughed and shook his head, ready to nix that notion. He wouldn't even go there in a cover-up. He leaned on another answer—one that could be true. "I don't see that happening anywhere in the near future. Or even the far future. But my little sister is graduating college soon, so I thought I might get her a little something. What's a good graduation gift?"

The bearded man walked behind the counter, unlocked a glass case, and gestured to several diamonds that could be set into a bracelet or earrings. "Surely, a lovely pair of simple diamond earrings would be a wonderful gift for your sister as she embarks on her first job after college. They say *classy and elegant*, and what employer wouldn't want that?"

Jake rested his elbows against the counter, taking in the sea of sparkling gems that shimmered like brilliant reflections. "So many to choose from. What do other customers get?"

The man reached into the case for a handful of small diamonds, and he sprinkled the gems on a swath of black velvet. "These are very popular. And the price is incredibly reasonable."

Jake nodded, as if considering his purchase. He screwed up the corner of his lips. "Business is good these days?" he asked casually as he studied one of the gems. "I keep hearing all about diamonds in the Caymans."

The man nodded vigorously and gestured to the door. More customers were starting to stream in. "Business has never been better. Sometimes it's so good I can't even handle it. I am a lucky man to work here. The only thing that would make me luckier would be if I can beat my brother at darts someday."

Jake cracked up, thinking of his dart coach from last night. "Is that so?"

The man nodded. "Oh yes. He plays a mean game of darts."

"As a matter of fact, I got some pointers last night from a lovely lady. It's all about the angle," Jake said, then raised his arm and mimed tossing a dart.

The man nodded approvingly. "I shall try that next time."

Jake flashed him a smile, then snapped his fingers as if he'd just remembered something. "Say. Do you happen to have any of those diamonds with a sort of bluish tint to them? A very faint blue glow?"

The man shook his head. "Ah, sorry to say I do not. Those are quite special. One of my colleagues down the street at International Diamonds has some from time to time. A few months ago, he handled a small batch of them for a new customer, who brought them in from the United States. International Diamonds is where you want to go for a stone like that. He might even have one or two left over from that batch."

Ding, ding, ding!

"Excellent," Jake said, reining in a grin and extending a hand to shake. "I appreciate that. And I'll be back to pick one up for my sister soon. What's your name?"

"Wilder."

"Nice to meet you, Wilder."

The man bowed once more, then headed over to his new customers as Jake took off.

⁓

As Jake walked away from the shop, he grabbed his phone and called up that e-mail from his case file—the one Andrew's IT guy had resurrected from the deleted folder.

Jake scrubbed a hand across his chin as he studied it once more. The note referenced an amount. The sender discussed safe transport. But there was no mention of paintings or art, specifically.

The luxury good itself had gone unnamed. Andrew had suspected art given Eli's affinity for it, as well as his fiancée's business venture.

Perhaps the e-mail was about art. But maybe it was *actually* about something else. After all, how many $5,000 paintings did you have to move to equal $10 million? A fuck ton, that was how many. And paintings took up a helluva lot more space on a plane than gems did. Especially when they required safe transport.

Jake's instincts were telling him something. To pay attention to the little details, too—the name of Eli's nightclub, the bling on the woman, the tint of the diamonds, and the timing of the jewel trade.

Was Eli ferrying something else entirely from the United States to the Caymans?

He called Andrew and ran the new possibility past him.

"My team is still working on deciphering those other documents to see if we can get any more intel, but I'm looking at the e-mail now to Constantine," Andrew said in a focused tone. "And if that's what he took to the Caymans, they'd be the rightful property of the Eli Fund."

"Let's get 'em back, then."

"Let's do it."

Jake located International Diamonds, a sprawling shop that occupied a huge street corner. The sign said OPEN TOMORROW.

Looked like he was free to rendezvous with the mermaid for now.

CHAPTER NINE

Her stepfather held his arms out wide, beaming as Steph walked up the steps to Tristan's, his favorite brunch spot on the island. No surprise that brunch was his favorite meal. That was a fitting choice for a man who liked the finer things in life. Wine, art, caviar, trips, and very pretty women.

But he also liked his kids. He practically bounced on his sandaled feet as Steph headed to him. The second she reached the top step, he wrapped his arms around her and held her close.

Like he'd missed her.

Like she was his precious girl.

She caught a faint whiff of his woodsy aftershave, a familiar scent from her youth. His arms wrapped around her were the definition of safety. So many times growing up, he'd comforted her with a hug when she'd fallen, gotten hurt, lost a game, and so, some kind of muscle memory kicked in as he embraced her.

Family.

She'd never known her own father. Eli was as close as she'd ever come to a dad. Perhaps that's why the way it ended hurt even more, knowing he'd absconded with the money her mom had given him to start his business. Steph's brain told her Eli was a con man, a thief. Trouble was that standing there in his strong, warm hug, she desperately wanted her brain to be wrong. How could she love and loathe this man so much at once? Her muscles tensed with simmering frustration over how he'd hurt the person she loved most at the same damn time that she was actually happy to see him, too. She was tired of the push-and-pull tug-of-war inside her heart, of trying to sort the truth from the lies. If she was to have any peace, she had to find out which was the real Eli.

"It's been too long," he declared, breaking the embrace and dropping his hands to her arms, smiling widely as he seemed to drink her in. "You don't look a day over twenty. How old are you now? Eighteen? Fifteen?"

"Eli," she said, rolling her eyes.

"I know you're twenty-eight, sweetheart. Let's catch up on everything. I want to hear every detail of what you've been up to," he said, and in mere seconds, the maître d' swooped by and seated them at the best table on the terrace. The restaurant had just opened for brunch and was already bustling.

As soon as he walked away, the restaurant owner marched over and beamed. "Hello again, Mr. Thompson," he said.

"Good to see you, Tristan. I'm still noodling on our conversation from this morning."

"Excellent. Let it marinate some more. As long as you need. I do think it can be good for both of us." The tall, salt-and-pepper-haired man turned to Steph and dropped a chaste kiss on her cheek. "And welcome back, Miss Steph. What a pleasure to see you again, too."

"Thank you so much, Tristan. I see you're as busy as ever," she said, flashing a quick smile to the man she'd known for years—a local friend of her stepdad's.

"I can't complain one bit," he said, handing them menus, then bowing briefly before he scuttled away.

"Can't complain my butt," Eli muttered.

She arched an eyebrow in question.

"He complains about everything," Eli whispered.

"Are you doing business with Tristan?" Steph asked.

Eli flicked open his cloth napkin and waved it once, before spreading it across his lap. "Potentially. He wants me to back a new venture of his, but then again, doesn't everyone?" he said, with an *it's-good-to-be-the-king* look in his eyes.

"I don't know. Does everyone?" she asked drily, her lips quirking up as she teased him.

"Some days, my dear, it seems that way. Everyone lining up to ask for a little of this, a little of that," he said, rubbing his thumb across two fingers.

"Do you ever say yes?" she asked as she spread a champagne-colored napkin over her lap.

He lowered his voice to a thread. "Rarely. I'm actually trying to be retired. To devote my energy to my charitable endeavors."

She furrowed her brow. Two things didn't add up. She'd never known him to be terribly interested in charity, plus, he was still working. "But you run a nightclub," she said, zeroing in on one logical fallacy.

"The club is hardly work. That's nothing but passion. I'm usually there in my office every day at this time, and it feels like pure pleasure."

"The club is doing well, I hear," she said, damn curious if the missing money had funded his passion.

"It is. You should come by and see it. Dance a little, feel the Sapphire energy. It's wonderful. Come by tonight. Jane Black is in town, and she'll be singing a few of her hit songs. I know you love her music."

A ping of excitement zipped through her. "I do love Jane Black," Steph admitted begrudgingly, because these moments made her mission tougher. He knew her likes, he knew her dislikes, he knew her.

"I know you do," he said with a smile. "So stop by. I'll make sure you're on the VIP list. I have to head over to Little Cayman tonight, so

I won't be there, but my manager, Ferdinand, is. If you need anything, he's the man with the snake tattoo on his left arm."

"Duly noted. Sounds like he'd be hard to miss, then. And I'm glad the club is doing well," she said, though that wasn't entirely true. If it were doing well at her mom's expense, *glad* wasn't the right word. The word rhymed with *glad*, though, and had an *as hell* following it.

"It's a dream nightclub," Eli said. "Plus, it feeds my charity work. I donate all my profits."

"You do? That's really great," she said with a brief smile. She'd never known this side of him, the charitable one.

"Indeed. I have many causes I support, but for now, look at the menu. Everything is amazing, as you know."

A few minutes later, a waiter arrived with glasses of water and to take their orders. Eli chose a mimosa and eggs benedict, while Steph opted for eggs and toast.

"You should get a quiche. Or a salmon omelet. Don't get something you can eat at a diner," he said.

"I wasn't aware that eggs and toast were gauche diner food. But I've filed that away now," she said, tapping her temple as the waiter left.

"That's not it. I just want you to enjoy yourself. You should always enjoy yourself when you're with me," he said, tucking his hands under his chin and shaking his head in admiration. "I can't believe you're really here. You're sure you're not just an apparition? A figment of my happy imagination?" he said, waving a hand like a magician with a scarf.

My God, that's what the man was—a damn wizard. So charming. So ebullient. Pretty much the happiest person you'd ever meet in your life.

"It's really me. In the flesh," she said, gesturing to herself like she was posing for a selfie.

"I'm simply delighted. Do you have any idea how happy it makes me to hear from you?"

"A lot?" she asked playfully, letting herself enjoy this moment.

"More than I can even measure," he said, reaching for his glass. "Tell me everything. How is your company? Is that jerk who tried to hurt your tour business suffering?"

"I don't know. I don't talk to Duke, so I don't have a good sense on a scale of one to ten of his daily suffering."

"Let's hope it's a ten," he said, narrowing his eyes and brandishing his teeth, as if he were ready to gnash Duke to a bloody pulp. "I wish you'd have let me help you with that fiasco."

Steph gaped at him, staring at him like an oddity. "You didn't offer," she pointed out incredulously, because she wasn't going to let him play revisionist historian.

"You didn't ask," he said.

Touché.

"Fair enough," she said. "Besides, my mother helped me out, and I've been rebuilding."

"Good. I'm thrilled." He leaned back in his chair and glanced briefly at the crowds click-clacking by—businessmen and -women streaming in and out of banks. "But do you need anything now?" He waved broadly behind him. "My bank is right over there."

She shook her head. "Thank you, I'm good. And speaking of my mom, there's something I wanted to bring up," she said, straightening her spine, readying for her mission. This was why she came to the Caymans early. To right a wrong, and the simplest way to do that was to ask.

After all, he'd given her the permission seconds ago.

He raised his eyebrows, waiting.

She drew a quiet breath, letting it fill her lungs, with strength, she imagined. Then, calmly, she asked, "I have a request. There's something I'd like you to do."

He cocked his head. "Of course. What is it?"

He sounded so damn genuine. Like he really would do anything she asked.

His eager reply further emboldened her.

"It's about the money Mom invested in your fund when you started it. I think you should pay her back. You would never have had the hedge fund without her. She made it possible for you to start a business that made you rich. It's only fair to return the seed money, especially now that you've retired," she said, making her argument crisp and clear, laying out the facts.

But his response was a dismissive laugh. "That's silly, dear. She has her jewelry sales."

Her brow knit together. Seriously? That was his answer? She shoved aside the curl of annoyance in her gut, keeping her voice even as she tried again. "Eli, she helped you in a big way when you needed her, and she's trying to rebuild her business now after the divorce. Don't you think it would be the right thing to do with the money?"

"She doesn't need *my* money if she's busy selling jewelry again. She's always been so talented with her little artsy tinkering."

His money? Ha. The jury was out on whether it was even his money at all. "Her *little artsy tinkering?* Her little artsy tinkering funded your company that you just retired from. And you made sure she got *nothing* in the divorce," she said, a bead of anger coiling through her. Screw her sentimental heart. Her brain quickly erased the question of which Eli was real. He was a rat bastard right now, but if she didn't get ahold of her roiling emotions soon, her recon mission would go bust.

She reminded herself to breathe. To focus on her prana or something. Whatever that was.

Eli waved a hand in the air, erasing it all. "Bah, that's crazy. It was a completely fair settlement. But let's not talk of such unpleasant matters, my dear. Look, our brunch is here," he said, his eyes lighting up as a new waiter served them their plates.

"Hey, Steph," the waiter said as he set down her eggs. She glanced up to see a guy who had helped out at Devon's from time to time was serving them. His eyes sparkled brightly.

"Good to see you, Reid," she said, rising to give him a quick hug. "What have you been up to? Did you ever get the boat you had your eye on?"

"I did. I'm hoping to start a charter fishing business soon," he said, and her mind flicked back to Jake. Maybe someday, Jake would return to this island and charter a fishing boat from this waiter.

"You'll have to let me know if you do, so I can refer tourists to you."

"That would be excellent," he said with a wide smile. He turned to her stepfather and gestured to his food. "Bon appétit, Mr. Thompson. It's always a pleasure to see you here at Tristan's."

"And you as well, Reid." When he walked away, her father tipped his forehead to the waiter. "Everyone here loves you. You really should move here."

"Yes, I should. But I like Miami, too. Because I like my mother. She's not the kind of person who hurts someone she loves," she said, her voice calm, her tone deliberately low. But her eyes locked with his as she aimed to deliver a crystal-clear message.

He picked up his fork and looked at her, speaking firmly. "What happened between your mother and me is between us. We've put it behind us. Let's you and I do the same. Let's move on and forge a new relationship."

Her jaw dropped as she reached for a piece of toast. "Are you kidding me? It's behind you and her? Hardly."

"It absolutely is. Shelly and I have moved on. So let's focus on other matters," he said, digging into his eggs benedict.

"Eli, you need to play fair. Why can't you at least return the money she funded your firm with?"

"Sweetheart," he said, admonishing her.

"Or is that money someplace else?" she asked, pressing the issue, refusing to let it go.

"Steph. Let's have a nice meal together," he said, taking time to punctuate each word. He pointed to her plate and her untouched food.

"Eat your eggs and toast. And let's set a time for dinner. I want you to meet Isla."

"Is that your new girlfriend?" she asked as she picked up her fork.

"Fiancée. And she's amazing," he said as he finished chewing. "You'll love her," he said, his voice laced with admiration and reverence. "I feel like she's my soul mate."

Steph wanted to gag, or pretend to gag. Just so he could see how ridiculous he sounded. Yet, she also knew that he meant it. The man fell in love at the drop of a hat and was convinced every woman he screwed was the love of his life.

"That's great," she said through clenched teeth. She bit into her toast so she wouldn't accidentally spew words of utter frustration all over the table.

"You know what's really great? We connect on every level. *It* has never been better," he said, whispering as he waggled his eyebrows at the word *it*. *Oh Lord. Oh dear. Please stop.* "At my age, too! Can you believe it?"

"It's truly astonishing," she said, deadpan, as he simply beamed in amazement of his own supposed prowess.

"I'm just a lucky son-of-a-bitch. To have love and passion like this. Have you ever just had that kind of instant chemistry with someone?" he asked, snapping his finger.

Her mind wandered briefly to yesterday, and the way Jake had pressed his hard body against hers by the wall. Her stomach loop-the-looped like a hang glider as sparks raced through her. Their chemistry was instantaneous. It was electric. She craved more of it and hoped he'd follow the trail of clues to find her again this afternoon. If he did, perhaps they could explore more of their chemistry.

Wait.

She shouldn't be thinking about him while talking to her stepdad. She certainly didn't want to be lusting after Jake in the same breath as Eli waxed on about his bedroom escapades.

Time to press the brakes.

She held up her palm. "Glad you're happy. But I really don't need to know the details."

"Of course not. I've said too much about private affairs. But Isla is a giver. Oh, does she ever love to give," he said, and the look in his eyes as he seemed to drift off momentarily had Steph strongly considering jet-packing her way out of here. He stopped to reach into his pocket. "Speaking of giving, Isla wanted me to give this to you. She can't wait to meet you."

He set a small black box on the table. The size gave it away. So did his history. He tapped his manicured finger against the jewel box, then gently nudged it across the white linen tablecloth. A soft breeze blew across the terrace, and Steph tucked a strand of hair behind her ear.

"Eli," she said softly, shaking her head, as if she could erase the prospect of a gift she really shouldn't take. "You don't need to do this."

"Open it," he commanded.

Her heart beat erratically. She couldn't take a gift from him. Not now. Not with these questions hanging over her, weighing like a heavy anchor on her heart.

"Please open it," he urged.

She clicked open the box and gasped. My God, it was gorgeous. She was ashamed at how she nearly salivated at the sight. Glittering on a white silk bed was a stunning diamond.

"I didn't have it set yet or placed on a chain. I thought, if you like it, we can have it added to your treasure chest," he said, tipping his chin to her regular necklace.

She swallowed. Her mouth was dry. Shaking her head, she clicked the box closed and pushed it back toward him. "I can't take this."

"Nonsense. You can, and you will. It's a gift. Just because I'm no longer married to Shelly doesn't mean I don't care about you, my dear." He pushed it back to her side. She nudged it back to him. He slid it back to her. "Plus, for every diamond that comes from this mine, money is contributed to help build schools in Africa."

"That's nice to hear," she admitted.

Then, Steph's spidey senses tingled. Eli adored jewels. Loved them for their sparkle. Loved them for their ability to charm his mistresses. Hell, he'd given the same kind of gifts to them over the years—jewels. Diamond earrings. Ruby necklace. Gold bracelet. Jewelry had been his favorite thing to buy when she was younger.

Was jewelry still his pleasure?

He'd stolen money from his firm, her mother had told her.

Now, he had jewels.

Maybe she was overreaching, but her mind leaped several steps ahead. Had he somehow funneled all that money into jewels? Ferried the money out of the country in gems, like a drug mule?

Her stomach dived. She hoped against hope that this was simply a gift, even though she'd be stupid not to consider other possibilities.

"Thank you," she said quietly, taking the box. She wasn't taking it for herself, though. She was taking it to study it. To learn if it was part of his pirate's booty. "It's quite lovely."

"Wonderful. So you'll come over Thursday night? For dinner?" he asked, diving back into his meal.

She started to say no when she realized dinner might be the very best thing she could do. She'd been invited, and an invitation could lead to information.

"Sure. I would love to," she said as she reined in a grin. She fixed on a straight ruler mouth, though inside she wanted to punch the air. She was the inside woman with inside access now. This would be a slam dunk to learn the truth of the missing money.

"Fantastic. Isla is having some friends over, too," he said as he took a drink of his mimosa.

"Oh," she said, her ebullience fading. That didn't sound like the ideal occasion for intel gathering. Not with a gaggle of friends.

"Come at seven. My home is gorgeous. I can't wait for you to see it."

OK, maybe *this* could work.

"I can't wait to see it, either," she said.

And to explore it.

⌒⌒

As Jake headed up the steps to Tristan's, ready to do a little digging into what his target was up to, he did a double take. He spotted a man who looked like Eli standing up at a table on the terrace. A blonde in a jean skirt walked away from him, and those legs looked awfully familiar.

He froze like a statue.

What the hell?

Why would his Ariel be dining with Eli?

He had no answer.

He blinked, then unfroze. No time to linger. Time to act. He grabbed his phone to snap a photo of her from behind. As he walked out of her line of sight, he sent it to Andrew and inquired about any pretty blondes in Eli's life, leaving out the little detail that Jake had already acquainted himself with her lips yesterday evening. Nope. That nugget was tucked in his brain, and it was his alone for safekeeping.

When he glanced back, she was gone.

Time to make himself scarce, too.

CHAPTER TEN

Bubbles rose up in the crystal-blue water. A pair of turtles paddled through the shallow reef. The underwater creatures skimmed by her, the front leg of one sweeping along her skin.

Boy, had she missed these guys fiercely in the last year.

The big turtles with their wise faces and kind eyes had always seemed like kindred spirits when she was growing up in Miami, exploring the beaches and shallow waters off the coast of Florida. Gentle giants who wouldn't harm a fly. Swimming with the turtles had brought her a sense of serenity after her dad died. While she didn't remember him at all, she knew how his death had affected her mom and how sad her mom had been in the years that followed. Steph had been too young to understand her own emotional response, but now, years later, she saw that she'd turned to the ocean for comfort. Now, as she glided along the shallow bottom of Happy Turtle Cove, peace flowed through her veins once more. *A natural Prozac,* she'd called it during many of the guided dives she oversaw here in the early days of her business.

When Duke had lashed out at her, lobbing underhanded jabs and hooks, he'd hit the Caymans first, knowing her love of this land. He posted fake review after fake review under new names across all the online review sites, simply because she'd had the gall to leave him.

So cruel. So punishing.

Especially since no one had cheated, no one had strayed.

After three years together, their relationship had gone stale. Duke had been lazy, and aimless, and hadn't found a job in more than a year, but he also hadn't looked hard for one. He'd been content to live off Steph and the money she'd generated then from her business.

If she was going to take away his free ride, he was going to bring it down with him, so he'd hit her where it hurt. Her chest pinched with the unpleasant memories, then she reminded herself to live for the moment, to enjoy this peace and calm in the ocean with her favorite creatures.

In a few days, she'd be showing a group of tourists from Texas this very spot, introducing them to the world under the ocean and the array of marine life here.

Maybe these two turtles would return. That prospect of seeing them again made the past slink away and had the halo effect of pushing the odd encounter with Eli to the background. Spending time with him was like living in a fun house, with swaying floors and seesawing ramps. His odd sweetness, mixed with his utter cluelessness, topped with his misplaced generosity, turned her insides topsy-turvy.

After brunch, she'd dropped off the diamond at her hotel, locking it in her safe to keep it out of harm's way. Then, she headed here for some underwater therapy. Being below the sea reset her mind. As she swam, she let go of the morning encounter and focused on what was ahead. In a few minutes, if fate were on her side, she might see that handsome man again from last night. Anticipation skittered through her veins, along with that crazy thing known as hope. She had no idea if Jake would show. True, Marie had texted her last night letting her know she'd passed along the napkin message. But whether the fisherman would follow it was entirely unknown.

Steph kicked her finned feet and glided closer to shore, pushing up to the surface as she neared the sand.

Adjusting quickly to her land legs, she stood in the shallow waters, pushed her goggles onto her forehead, and took the snorkel out of her mouth. When she reached the sand, she dried off and tucked the snorkel gear in its bag. She grabbed a short cotton sundress and started to tug it over her head, then thought better of it. She'd pull it on once her bikini dried more.

She crossed her fingers and waited, hoping the sexy man would show up at Happy Turtle Cove at 1:23 p.m.

Right on time, he walked across the beach.

⁓

No fair. It was no fucking fair for her to be that hot.

He was going to call the Council of Hotness and ask for her membership to be revoked.

Because . . . *that bikini.*

He stood no chance. It was so damn revealing, what with being a bikini and all, and showcased all her assets. Those legs. That flat stomach. Those gorgeous breasts.

Wave the flag. Call the troops. Surrender was upon him.

"You deciphered my code," she said with an approving grin as he walked to her, his ankles digging into the white, sugary sand.

"One, I like codes. Two, I like challenges, and three, even without the punctuation between the numbers, I figured out you meant the time," he said, wishing it wasn't so damn easy to slide back into banter with her. Her smile was a lasso tossed around his waist that brought him to his knees.

"And you are incredibly punctual, too. Not gonna lie, Jake. Punctuality is super sexy," she said with a smile.

How on earth could a smile like that live on a liar?

Well, he didn't technically know if she was a liar.

All he knew was she'd had brunch with his target. Given Rosalinda's fake plays, that was enough to raise Jake's hackles. But he didn't have any hard-and-fast answers because Andrew was in a meeting, and Jake was still waiting to hear from his client on who this lovely woman was.

For now, he'd have to get to the bottom of this on his own, and figure out if he was being played by the woman with the starfish belly ring. He wasn't going to let last night's kiss cloud his focus. He wasn't going to let that blue bikini that hugged her hips, and had the good fortune to snuggle up to her breasts, distract him. Absolutely not.

"I'm glad you made it. I thought you'd get a kick out of Happy Turtle Cove, since you named me Happy Turtle," she said, then dropped her voice to a faux whisper. "But it's really a cove for turtles. I was just swimming with them."

Stop. Just stop.

Swimming with turtles was too adorable. Especially when her nose crinkled. A constellation of freckles was splashed across her nose. He hadn't noticed them yesterday. Briefly, he wondered where else she might be hiding freckles that he'd uncover on a proper and thorough investigation of her fantastic body. Preferably with his tongue, across every inch of her skin. "You were actually swimming with turtles?"

She tapped the mesh bag on her shoulder. "My snorkel gear is in here." She gestured to her body. "Sorry, I'm still in my bathing suit. I'll put on a sundress as soon as this is dry."

"Or just remove the bikini entirely so it'll dry faster. It's not ever necessary to put on a dress on my account. I'm completely OK with the bikini as a sole item of clothing on a woman like you," he said, then nearly smacked himself. He had to stop thinking with his dick. He had to use that head on his goddamn shoulders.

Cover up that body. Put a paper bag over your face. Stop being so damn sexy and sweet. Stop making me think about taking you back to my hotel room and peeling off that bikini and tasting how sweet your sun-kissed skin is.

"I'm glad to know that both nudity and skimpy bathing suits have your sartorial approval. But I actually hope to look somewhat decent when you take me to the Coconut Iguana. My friend Sandy runs it."

He arched an eyebrow in question.

She tapped her wrist, even though it was bare. She didn't strike him as a watch wearer. "Lunch time. I'm hungry. So I decided to let you take me out to lunch as a reward for your showing up and following my napkin instructions. Plus, they have the best fish tacos on the Islands, and absolutely amazing coconut drinks," she said, stepping closer and bumping her hip against him.

A groan rumbled in his chest. Why was the universe torturing him?

He forced his brain to take over. To focus on facts, not lust. Because it made no sense why she'd be hungry, since he'd seen her at a restaurant two hours ago, and she didn't look like she noshed around the clock. This was another sign that she might be working for the enemy.

"I'm hungry, too. Let's head to the Coconut Iguana." He held out a hand, telling himself that lunch was the perfect opportunity to get to the heart of who this woman was. Since she knew Eli, she might be a valuable asset. And if this woman was playing him, he could play her.

He was a pro.

He had skills.

He knew what he was doing.

She took his hand, and in a second all thoughts were erased when her lips crushed his. All skills and strategy and plans were swept to sea. Out of the blue, she went for it, sealing her delicious mouth to his and kissing him like she'd been reliving last evening's kiss, too. Like he had. That first kiss had made him want so much more.

This second kiss reminded him of why.

She wasn't tentative; she wasn't testing the waters. She was a determined woman—determined to consume him and devour all his will, all his reason, every last ounce of logic that was quickly slipping away in a kiss that fried his brain.

Ask him his name, he could barely remember.

Ask where he was, and he couldn't say.

All he knew was the taste of her lips and the feel of her warm body. He looped his arms around her nearly naked frame and yanked her close, taking the reins and kissing her like a hungry man. His hands lingered on her lower back for the briefest of seconds, traveling across her skin that was warm from the sun blazing brightly overhead. He trailed his fingertips lower, dropping one hand to her ass and squeezing a round, firm cheek. He groaned. A deep, hungry sound. He wanted this woman with a fierceness he hadn't felt in ages. He didn't even know her name.

Right now, nothing mattered but how fantastic she felt.

She pressed her lush body to his, lining up her belly against his hard-on and rubbing lightly against him. There might very well be families around. There might be legions of people watching them as she sighed sexily in his mouth and pressed into him. He didn't care. This was not an innocent kiss. It was a hot, dirty one. It was a prelude that demanded clothing be stripped off and bodies be tangled together. She curled her hands into his hair and practically clawed at his skull. In the ferocity of her grip, his restraint was reduced to a thread.

He broke the kiss for a split second and spoke in a ragged voice, full of lust. "I want to do bad things to you."

Her eyes lit up. "I like bad things. I want bad things."

She grabbed him and they kissed more. Harder. Rougher.

He pictured her in bed. Scratching his back. Digging her nails into his flesh. Holding on hard as he took her and fucked her through multiple toe-curling orgasms before he even allowed one for himself. He wanted to see her spread out, flush with desire, sated with the pleasure that he'd given her. He craved hearing her orgasmic cries and watching her come undone, over and over. He wanted to back her up against that palm tree right now, strip off those bikini bottoms, and explore her legs, taste her sweetness, feel her heat.

But he wanted to know her goddamn name, too. Not just how she felt coming undone.

Somehow, he managed to untangle himself from her. They were both panting. Her eyes were glossy with desire. He was sure his hair was a wild mess from her hands in it. He was equally sure he liked her hands in his hair.

He exhaled deeply and rubbed a hand across his jaw, trying to reset his mind. He clasped his hands together. "So now that I've nearly ripped off your clothes on the beach and had my tongue down your throat in a bar, perhaps you could tell me your real name."

"You don't think it's Ariel?" she asked coyly, her lips curving into a naughty grin.

"No," he said as she bent down for her dress and tugged it over her head. Turned out covering up didn't do much for his desire to have his hands all over her body. He still wanted her just as badly. Against his better judgment. "I'm pretty sure it's not Ariel. I'd love to know what it really is."

Or what new fake name you'll give me.

"Well, it does seem you've passed enough tests now to earn the name."

"Ah, so you have been testing me?"

She laughed and nodded. "I'm a twenty-eight-year-old woman living in a world where anyone gets burned online. You're a man with one name only who I met on an island. I'm not stupid. I'm also not Ariel, but my business is actually called Ariel's Island Eco-Adventure Tours. I run a tour business in the Caribbean," she said, and something about her job sounded vaguely familiar. It tickled his brain, nagging away at him. "I studied marine biology in college so I could lead dives and snorkel trips. I live in Miami, but I've been rebuilding my business here and in other places. I'm Steph Anderson and it is a pleasure to officially meet you."

He nearly stumbled. His jaw almost dropped. His eyes practically popped out of his head. But he fought back all those natural reactions because he didn't want to let on that he knew the name Steph, since he'd looked up the names of Eli's family before he arrived.

Including his stepchildren.

She stared at him. Then made a rolling gesture with her hand. "Your turn."

"Jake Harlowe," he said, and his voice sounded funny to him. Rougher than usual, etched with surprise that he needed to cover up. He spoke quickly. "Former army intelligence. Now I run a recovery business in Key Largo."

She grinned widely. "You're not far away from me."

"No. I'm not at all," he said crisply. He didn't want to get into the implications of hometown proximity. "Let's get you lunch."

"What's a recovery business?" she asked as they walked across the sand to the winding path along the beach. "Like information recovery? With computers?"

"Sort of. My job's woefully dull," he said, though that couldn't be further from the truth. "Tell me more about marine biology. That's fascinating. I've never met a marine biologist. That's the profession career counselors use when they go to schools and give gung-ho pep talks about all the vast possibilities of future jobs. When they cite interesting, cool, or unusual careers, marine biologist is up there with archaeologist."

"That's a conspiracy, actually, among marine biologists and archaeologists. To make sure we all seem super cool."

He laughed, wishing he didn't enjoy her company so much. He reminded himself that this lunch date wasn't a date. It was a mission. He was infiltrating the target.

That was all.

CHAPTER ELEVEN

A gull squawked as it swooped past the outside of the Coconut Iguana, hunting for leftovers.

The bird wouldn't find many at Steph's table. Only one tortilla was left on her plate and Jake had finished his tacos, declaring them some of the best he'd ever had. The meal had been fantastic, the view of the water even better, but the company was the best part. After that searing kiss—a full-body kiss if there ever was one—they'd settled into a late lunch and good conversation.

"See! I told you the fish tacos were yummy. My friend Sandy manages this place, and she told me the reason they taste so good is because of the coconut."

"Coconut in the fish tacos?" he said, and he clucked his tongue and nodded. "Come to think of it, they did taste like coconut. And hey, better than coconut water."

"Isn't it weird that coconuts can be so delish but coconut water isn't? And truth be told, I didn't eat much this morning when I went out because I knew I wanted you to take me here."

"So you saved your appetite for me," he said, raising an eyebrow.

"I did. Do you feel special?"

He laughed. "A little."

"Then I need to confess something."

He sat up straighter. His expression turned serious, his mouth now approximating a ruler. "What is it?" he asked, sounding breathless with anticipation.

"Look. I feel this is important that you know," she said, stopping to pause, then took a deep breath, preparing to drop a bomb on him. She lowered her eyes, as if embarrassed, then raised them, cupping her hand over the side of her mouth. "I'm not actually a marine biologist."

She frowned and adopted her best *sad puppy dog eyes.*

He flung his napkin on the table and pushed back in his chair. "That's it. I'm leaving," he huffed.

She stretched across the table and patted his chair. "But wait. I need you to know the full truth. I'm actually an archaeologist."

"Ah, that makes perfect sense," he said, his green eyes lighting up with laughter. "I take it you're on a hunt for a long-lost city buried under the sand?"

"Actually, there are some great wrecks here. In the water. Do you dive?"

He nodded. "I have."

"You should come with me, then. We can check out some boats from long ago."

He didn't answer her. He simply shrugged, which was an odd reaction, considering he'd been playing along with her previous remarks. But maybe she was pushing him by suggesting a dive, though that hardly seemed akin to a commitment request that would give a man the heebie-jeebies. Best to keep their conversation free and breezy. She barely knew him, so there was no point in suggesting another date yet, like a dive.

A bright green bird with an orange chin hopped on the railing at the bar and grill, searching for scraps. Steph tugged away at a section of her fish taco and dropped it on the railing.

Jake pointed to the sign on the wooden post: DON'T FEED THE BIRDS. "Scofflaw."

She raised an eyebrow. "I'm not afraid to break a few rules."

"Is that so? Tell me more about your lawlessness."

She tucked her hands under her chin. "One time when I was younger, my mom and stepdad took us to this fancy hotel in Hawaii, and my brother and I fed biscotti from my mom's coffee each morning to all the tropical birds at the window of our hotel room. Until housekeeping ratted us out, sent the manager to our room, and told us the other guests didn't like us feeding the birds. Translation: *bird poop*."

"Is this your way of telling me you're not an archaeologist, either? That you're an ornithologist?"

She laughed and shook her head. "What I meant was that I'm not technically a marine biologist—I just studied it in college. So I wanted you to know that I'm not technically an official '*marine biologist*,'" she said, sketching air quotes as she spoke.

She waited for some sort of witty retort from him, but it didn't come. She excused herself for a quick trip to the ladies' room, and when she returned he fired off another question.

"Did you know when you studied marine biology that you wanted to do that for a living?"

"All I knew was that I loved the water," she said, taking his questions as they came. "I could spend the whole day in the ocean and never want to come out. I might be part fish, come to think of it. I think I have scales on my legs," she said, and he smiled lightly, his eyes sparkling. She hoped the joke would lead them back to banter. But his grin didn't last for long.

"And you're a big fan of diving, too? Is that why you're here on this trip? To lead some dives?"

"Yes. I used to run a big business here, but I had some setbacks. Now it's growing again, and I love the Caymans. We used to come here a lot. And kiss stingrays."

"With your stepdad?"

She scrunched up her brow. "Yes, with him. But why would you ask that?"

He answered immediately. "You said just now he took you to Hawaii. And you said you've been here a lot. Seemed natural he might have done the whole stingray thing with you, too."

Something seemed odd about his comment, but she couldn't put a finger on it. Maybe what was odd was the lack of playful comments from him. But surely they'd pick up again, so she answered truthfully once more. "Yes, I did that with him."

"Is he here? On the Islands?"

That's when what felt so strange hit her—she'd done most of the talking at lunch. He was asking most of the questions. She straightened her spine and sat up taller, ready to ask him questions. She didn't want to be a conversational hog. She was digging his company and wanted to know more about him.

∽

She was simply too good to be true. There was no way she was for real. The playful humor, the casual conversation, the gorgeous figure, the love of the outdoors—clearly, she'd been tailor-made as his kryptonite to try to trip him up on a job. He was willing to bet she was planning on setting him up, just like Rosalinda had done.

His blood burned. He wished she'd just confess. Tell him she was tailing him.

"What about you. Are you really a recovery specialist? That just doesn't seem like you," she said, eyeing him up and down from the other side of the table.

How could she ask questions so naturally? She seemed so sure, so at ease. He was good at reading people and seeing through their lies. But he wasn't detecting any vibes that she was working the angles. Could she really not know who he was? Was there a chance she was simply the woman he kissed last night, and not out to trip him up on a job?

Before he knew the score, it was best to play it cool.

"Surprising, isn't it?" he answered, keeping up the banter as he tried to figure her out. "That such a rugged specimen of man could have such a dull job," he said, wondering briefly why he didn't just flat-out lie about his job. He'd met other women before and had never felt inclined to serve up the full truth. He'd often keep it vague and broad, saying he worked in security. But he wasn't giving her that line. He was coming as close as he could to the truth.

She laughed and pushed her sunglasses higher on her head. "See, Jake. I'd have pegged *you* as the archaeologist, like Indiana Jones. A rugged adventurer."

She didn't know the half of it.

"Hardly. But a man can dream," he said, then his phone blasted its ringtone for a client. The *Mission: Impossible* theme. "Give me one second."

"Of course."

Grabbing his mobile from the table, he saw Andrew's first name blasted across the screen. Shit. No way could he take this call now—not even to sneak out at the front of the restaurant. He couldn't risk her hearing him. He hit "Ignore," shrugging casually, like the call was not the damn one he'd been waiting for.

"Not your sister this time?"

"Just a client. I'll talk to him later." Coolly, he set his phone back down on the table.

"So, little sister gets Taylor Swift, and clients get *Mission: Impossible*? Cute," she said.

"Why thank you."

The phone buzzed, rattling on the wood. A text follow-up to the call. Jake stayed stoic. He wasn't going to pick it up. He didn't even glance at the phone.

"Sounds important," she said, tipping her forehead toward the device.

He shook his head. "But then we become a society where the little screen is more important than the post–fish taco conversation, and I just can't let that happen," he said with a small smirk, crossing his arms.

She rolled her eyes playfully. "Well, aren't you Mr. Manners."

"I do my best."

The phone shimmied once more, shaking in her direction. He remained impervious.

Steph laughed. "Just take it. It's fine. I don't mind," she said, then her hand darted out and she picked up the phone to give it to him.

He took it.

But she must have spotted the screen, because she tilted her head to the side, her gaze fixing on the screen. "Why is your client sending you a photo of me?"

Fuck.

Time to improvise. He shrugged casually and flashed a lopsided grin as he tucked his phone into his pocket. "'Cause you're—"

But she cut him off, and the word out of her mouth surprised him.

CHAPTER TWELVE

"Duke," she hissed.

The name burned her tongue. She narrowed her eyes as she hunched away from the table. "Are you a friend of Duke's?"

It was all she could imagine. That this was a sick new wrinkle in his smear campaign. That somehow he'd sent a friend to seduce her in some cruel fresh twist, then claim in a spate of horrid reviews that Ariel's Island Eco-Adventure Tours was run by no Disney princess, but by some kind of slut.

OK, fine. Maybe that was a stretch. But why on earth would Jake, the man she met less than twenty-four hours ago, have a photo of her face on his phone? He hadn't snapped any shots of her that she was aware of.

"Duke?" he asked as the waitress appeared.

"Sandy said dessert's on her if you want it," the waitress said, clasping her hands together as if this was the best news ever.

Normally, free dessert was damn good news.

But she was thrown, tossed in uncertain waters, and she couldn't read the man across from her to figure out if she should stay or go. Jake's expression was stony. He hardly seemed rattled, while Steph was nearly shaking. They were surrounded by handfuls of other diners, nibbling on fish tacos, drinking tropical drinks, passing the warm afternoon hours on the deck of a bar and grill. She wished she could be as laid-back as everyone else.

Including her date.

"How about a slice of mango cake with the scoop of coconut ice cream?" Jake said to the waitress, gesturing to the chalkboard menu hanging by the bar advertising today's specials. "I can't resist ice cream."

"Yes, we'll share it," Steph added, determined now not to let him be the only cool, collected one. If he could play at mango cake détente, so could she.

"One mango cake coming right up," the waitress said with a chipper tone and a happy swing of her elbow. She swiveled around and weaved through the tables on her way to the kitchen.

"Seriously. Who are you?" Steph said as she crossed her arms. "And why did someone send you a picture of me?"

"Who is Duke?" he countered.

She was undeterred. If Jake had anything whatsoever to do with the asshole who tried to take down her business, she needed to know now. "I bet he sent you that shot of me," she said, then reached out her hand, as if she could somehow grab his phone, even though he'd slid it inside his pocket.

Jake laughed and shook his head. "One, I don't know who Duke is. Two, whoever he is, he didn't send me your picture. Three, I have it, as I was saying before, because you're hot."

She furrowed her brow. "What? How does that compute?"

"Simply. Quite simply," he said, reaching for his glass of water and taking a gulp.

She waited expectantly for an answer, even as worry thrummed through her. "How so?"

"Do you have a little sister?"

"No," she answered quickly, wondering where this line of questioning was going.

"Well, I do, as you know. And she happens to be one of those wonderfully persistent sisters who wanted to know what I was doing last night, and I mentioned I had met a woman."

She arched her eyebrow. "And she sent you a photo of me?"

He nodded. "She did. She's like that. She also sent me an emoticon of lips smooching."

Despite her simmering annoyance, her lips quirked up. Because that was kind of cute. "She did?"

He shrugged casually. "Like I said, she likes to razz me. But I don't mind."

"Fine. But why would she send you a picture of me?"

"She broke me down. That's her special skill. She weaseled your name out of me when you were in the ladies' room a little while ago. I was texting her, and she just sent me back the photo she found of you online."

Hmmm.

His story added up. Mostly. Still, caution reigned, but she figured the fastest way to the truth was to lay her cards on the table.

"Scout's honor? Because I've been burned, Jake. You seem like a good guy, and I like spending time with you so far. I just want to know for certain that Duke has nothing to do with this," she said, gesturing from him to her, and the awareness that he was the first guy she'd had a date with since Duke made her throat hitch. "Promise?" she asked, her tone pleading, her voice threatening to break.

⌐୭

Maybe it was that quiver in her voice. Perhaps it was the way her eyes looked wet, like she was about to cry. It might even have been how scared she sounded. Whatever it was, he felt like shit now, especially given how he'd stretched the Kylie text into a big, fat white lie. He wished he didn't have to fib so blatantly, but how was he to trust her? But he hated, absolutely hated, seeing a woman in this state.

"Duke isn't involved. I swear. I don't even know who he is. Who is this guy?" he asked, trying to be as gentle as he could. Then he stiffened as the possibility smashed into him. "Is he your boyfriend?" he asked, bracing himself.

She scoffed. "No—God, no. He's an ex, though, and he tried to ruin my business. He enlisted a bunch of his friends to help him, too. That's why the picture made me worry that you were connected with him, or who knows what," she said, her voice still tough as she talked about the ex. But then it softened momentarily, and she whispered, "But I'm glad the picture just came from your sister. I think that's sweet."

Oh fuck.

His heart lurched toward her.

He was a schmuck. She was too sweet. She was too lovely. He was the asshole for not telling her the truth. He closed his eyes briefly, then opened them and tried to figure out what the hell to say. He didn't want to ruin the job he'd been hired for, but he didn't want to be a liar. That wasn't the guy he was teaching his younger siblings to be. That wasn't the man he wanted to be with a woman. He parted his lips to come clean, when she pointed to his phone.

"Can I see the picture she sent? You know, just to make sure it's not a hideous one?"

He laughed. "Now, how could you possibly take a hideous photo?"

She tilted her head to the side and made a monster face, or maybe it was a zombie face, as she scowled and hissed. "Like that?"

He held up a hand. "Fine. Fine. That would indeed be a hideous picture, and I guarantee the one on my phone is not."

Jake's radar was quiet, but he still wasn't sure if he was being played, so he kept on his armor of self-protection. But if she was being truthful, he didn't want to blow it by treating her like an asshole. Like her ex had done.

He grabbed his phone from his pocket and cautiously swiped his finger across the screen. He clicked on the image from the text so it downloaded to his gallery, then he opened it, widening it so it spread across the screen. He turned the phone to show her. "See? No zombie monster face here. All hot. All gorgeous. Are we good?"

She studied it from her side of the table. "Hmm."

"Hmm what?" he asked carefully.

"She got that from my website, right?"

The tiniest bit of heat spread across his cheeks as he tensed momentarily. Then he rolled the dice. "Yes," he said, hoping to hell and heaven and back that Andrew had snagged the shot from her site.

"Ah, that is so cute that your sister looked me up for you," she said sweetly, then in the blink of an eye, she swiped a finger across the screen, right to the last call received.

He yanked his phone back. But not in enough time. Because she'd removed her own phone from her purse and started to dial.

"Who are you calling?" he asked, his heart beating wildly with worry.

Her tone went from sweet to tough. "Just the number of the person who texted you the picture of me that's not on my website. That's on my personal Facebook page," she said, then her eyes widened when she stared at her own screen.

No, *gawked* was the better word.

Her jaw had dropped, and she whispered, *"Andrew?"* when the name of his client auto-filled on her screen.

His heart fell. *Shit. This was it.* He was about to lose the job when Andrew found out that he'd blown his cover. Damn it to hell. He had to stop letting his too-soft heart get in the way of work.

She stabbed at her phone and ended the call. She pointed at him. Her eyes were judge and jury. "I don't need to talk to him. I know who you are."

"You do?"

"You're the guy Andrew hired to find out about the money he thinks my stepdad stole. I have his number because I did a dive tour for him a few years ago, and my mom is friends with him."

"Your mom is friends with him?" he repeated, stalling, buying time, backpedaling however he could, when the waitress arrived with a small plate with a slice of cake on it, a scoop of ice cream on top. "Your mango cake," she said, then placed two forks next to it.

He reached for one, but Steph dropped her hand on his and squeezed when the waitress left. Her tone shifted once more, this time to a curious one. "Jake Harlowe, 'fess up. Are you the guy my stepdad's former business partner hired to find out what happened to the money? Because I think you are, and I want the same things. The truth. I know something bad happened, and it somehow involved Eli, and I'm pretty sure it also involves—"

They both answered at the same time, "—diamonds."

CHAPTER THIRTEEN

She pointed at him. He pointed at her.

"Are you working for Andrew?" he asked.

She shook her head. "I'm not working for anyone. I took this upon myself, but my mom told me Andrew hired someone, and clearly that someone seems to be you, judging from the picture on your phone of me that I highly doubt is from your sister and I'm willing to bet is from *your* client and my mom's friend."

"You appointed yourself private detective?"

She nodded. A burst of pride surged through her. She'd already tracked down some useful intel and had started putting clues together. "I did. I came down here a few days early to see what's going on with the money. But wait. Let's rewind. Why did you just say diamonds?"

"Because I saw one on Eli's fiancée, and the evidence is pointing in that direction."

Suddenly, the diamond in her safe seemed a lot *hotter* than it had this morning. Had her stepdad actually given her a gift from the stolen money? She'd tangoed with the possibility when she saw him, but now it seemed more plausible.

And more poisonous.

"So you and I are both trying to figure out what he's doing with the money, and maybe if that money is in diamonds? And you have evidence?"

"I do."

She wanted to know what he had, but something else gnawed at her brain. Something that warned her not to trust him. The part that had been burned. "Wait. You've lied to me so far, and now you're here clearly trying to get closer to me because you think I know something. Is that why you're having lunch with me today? Is that why you found me at the Pink Pelican last night?"

He sighed heavily and shoved a hand through his hair, like a bulldozer. "No. No. No. I didn't find you last night. I didn't know who you were at all. And besides, if you may recall," he said, tapping his chest, "I was at the Pink Pelican already. *You* walked in."

Damn, he made a good point. He hadn't been following her last night, and she was the one who'd left the trail of clues behind for him today. Chalk one up in his favor in the honesty column. "Fine. True," she admitted. "But don't you see how this looks? Like you knew who I was and you were trying to get info from me."

"Here's the reality. I saw you at the bar, thought you were stunning. We talked, we kissed, we had a good time. This was all totally separate from the job, because I didn't have a clue who you were last night. I wanted to see you again, plain and simple. Hell, I didn't even know your name. Then, I happened to spot you at breakfast with your stepdad at Tristan's—"

"You were following me?"

"No. I was in the area doing some recon work," he said, his voice firm, making it clear he didn't like her accusation. "Anyway, when I saw you finishing breakfast with him, I asked Andrew who you were. He told me, and now it turns out we're both, for all intents and purposes, working for the same people. You on your own for your mom. Me for Andrew. We're both looking out for the people who got screwed. I only made up the part about my sister texting me your photo. Everything else was true, especially the part about my telling her I met a woman last night who I wanted to see again."

She let his words soak in. She liked the ones where he said he wanted to see her again, because she'd sure wanted to see him, too. She'd been lingering over all the possibilities of him before she even saw him today. Still, she felt tricked. "You're saying none of that last night at the bar was an act? What about the kiss on the beach? Was that an act?"

He laughed loudly and shook his head. He gestured to his lap. "Did it feel like an act? Did you think I was faking it? That it was a few stuffed socks in my pants?"

She pressed her lips together, fighting hard to resist chuckling. "No, it didn't feel like a sock. But is a hard-on evidence that you didn't set me up?"

"What did I set you up for? Tell me. What on earth am I setting you up for?" he asked, holding his arms out wide. "I had an amazing time last night. Kissing you rocked my world, and I wanted more." He paused, then leaned closer and lowered his voice to a rough and sexy whisper. *"A lot more."*

A shiver ran down her spine, heating her up and turning her on in seconds. "I wanted more, too," she said, and he locked eyes with her, looking at her as if he were picturing her naked. She liked him looking at her that way. "I want all the bad things."

"I'm very good at doing bad things," he said in a rough, dirty tone. She dug her fingernails into her palms so she wouldn't launch herself across the table and ride him hard here at the restaurant.

OK, she really wouldn't do that. But maybe grab him and tug him into the ladies' room and pull him snug against her. Let him grab her wrists, pin them over her head, hike up her dress, and just take her. It had been so long, and she was willing to bet he could deliver everything she wanted.

But even so, she didn't know how to trust Jake, or anyone for that matter. She drop-kicked all those naughty thoughts away. "I'm sure you are quite skilled in the dirty department, but you're really telling me none of this was planned?" she asked, narrowing her eyes, maintaining her skeptical stare.

"Look, things got complicated today when I learned who you were. I'm not going to deny that. But I'm still here. Still talking to you." He tapped the table with his finger. "Because, maybe, we should work together to find the jewels. We're on the same team."

Her body said, *"Yes."* Her brain said, *"Don't be stupid, girl."* She wouldn't be fooled by lust. She had to remain focused. "Why should I work with you? What do I need from you? I'm the one who was invited into Eli's house later this week. I can just find them myself. I don't have to, you know, *break in*," she said, whispering the last words sarcastically. She might want the man, but that didn't mean she was going to team up with someone she just met twenty-four hours ago.

"What if they're not there?" he suggested casually. "What if they're, say, in the nightclub?"

"Then I'll find them there," she said, though admittedly, her task would be harder if they were in Sapphire. Still, she needed to stay the course and do this on her own. Maybe she wouldn't find a big, huge bag of diamonds. But perhaps she could find a way to get back her mom's money and even unearth evidence that Eli wasn't the man who'd so coolly dismissed her reasonable request at brunch. She wanted him to be the man who'd hugged her, who'd reminded her that he would have helped her business if she had asked. That's who she'd known him to be, and he'd shown her that inkling today. She held tight to it. Dipping her hand into her bag, she fished for some bills and set them on the table. "I'd better go. I have work to do."

As she stood, a willowy redhead appeared.

"Steph!"

"Sandy!"

Sandy wrapped her in a hug. "So good to see you. I missed you around here."

"I missed you, too," she said.

"I want to hear everything that's going on."

"Yes, me, too. We have to get together."

"A bunch of us are having a party on a friend's boat later this week. Want me to text you the details? Penny is off camping, but she should be back then."

"That sounds great. I'll be there."

"We can catch up and you can see the whole crew." Sandy squeezed her arm, then held up her finger. "It is *so* good to see you, and I'll be back. I need to run to the storage room. But stay here."

As Sandy scurried off, Jake met her gaze. The look in his eyes was one of satisfaction. He tipped his forehead to the disappearing Sandy. "That's why."

༄

He had an idea. He had a plan. It was crazy, but they might be able to kill two birds with one stone. Though he vastly preferred to work solo, especially given the Rosalinda fiasco, he had a hunch that he was going to need Steph on his side. This feisty, fiery woman wasn't going to step out of the picture on her own, not when she was motivated by personal reasons to hunt the diamonds. If Jake let her walk away, he'd keep running into her and butting heads. She was in a unique position to be his best weapon in this case. Better to work with her than against her.

He just needed her to see the benefits, and he didn't mean the physical ones, because tearing each other's clothes off needed to stop. ASAP. Besides, she seemed closer to throat-punching him than yanking off his shirt.

"Teaming up makes sense for us both."

"Why?"

"You need me and I need you. You know everyone on this island, which is great," he said, giving her his best pitch for why she'd want to work with him. "But it also means that people recognize you. It only took you going out to one breakfast with your stepdad for me to find out who you were. But me? No one knows me. I could be anyone. I can go places you can't go. I can be unseen. You have inside access, but I can walk around unnoticed."

She crossed her arms. Her lips were doing an excellent impression of a straight line. "Unless I told my stepdad who you were."

He scoffed and stared hard back at her, calling her bluff. "I highly doubt you'd do that."

"Why do you doubt me?"

"Because you want the same thing. You want to know what happened to the money. And I'm willing to bet you've already asked him, and he hasn't given you the answer you want." Her eyes widened, telling him he was right. "Am I right?" he asked, softer this time.

"Yes," she muttered.

"OK, so let's try to get the real answers."

She raised her face. "Show me, then. Show me this evidence," she said, her voice both strong and wavering. He could tell she was torn, but there was no doubt in his mind.

With his phone very tightly in his grip, he showed her the e-mail, giving her time to read it. He walked her through all the backstory, showing her some of the other documents, from how the date of the e-mail matched dates when money was moved from the fund, letting her take in the full scope of the crime.

She winced as if she'd just eaten something sour, then she blinked several times.

"We don't know for sure he stole anything," she said, desperation coloring her tone. "Just that he was in contact with someone. The only thing I know for sure is he screwed over my mom. That doesn't make him a criminal, just a man."

As far as Jake was concerned, Eli was 100 percent guilty and then some, but Steph was clinging to some shred of hope. It pained him to see her like his, but he had to think like a mercenary, not a man who would bend too easily to a vulnerable woman, so he made a lateral move.

"That's the evidence I'm working off of, and my job is to get this ten million and return it. You're still looking into the missing money, too. We can work together and finish faster. Join forces. We both bring something to the table."

She huffed, returning to her tough-girl persona. "Fine. That may be true, but I was the one who was invited into Eli's house," she said, tapping her chest. "In-vi-ted. Me. I'll just be strolling through the door on Thursday night, and I can wander around and check it out."

"Oh right. Of course," he said, deadpan, nodding several times for effect. "Because he probably keeps a bowlful of diamonds on his desk."

She shot him a side-eyed stare. "Ha ha, funny guy. But for your information, *no*. I don't think my stepdad treats them like jelly beans," she said, miming dipping her fingers into a bowl and grabbing some. "The point being, I can get the lay of the land. How many places can there be to hide diamonds in a house?" she said, in a tone full of bravado. It was, admittedly, adorable. Especially as she straightened up in her chair, acting all cool and tough. "I'll see if there's a loose floorboard somewhere. Or a piece of art hiding a safe behind it."

That's when he knew he had her. When he knew his plan would reel her in. She was, by her own admission, *playing private detective.* He was, by his profession, making a living as one. She had moxie and access, and he needed both, but he had something to offer her—*skills.* "When you find this floorboard, will you just yank it up with the hammer you keep in your back pocket?"

She breathed in sharply, and he was sure she was biting back all the things she didn't want to say. She snapped her gaze away from him and stared off the deck at the water and the waves gently rippling along the shore. The blue waters lapped the sand, and as she watched them, her expression seemed to soften. When she turned back to him, she lowered her voice. "Maybe I do keep a hammer in my back pocket. It's not as if I'm incapable."

"I don't think you're incapable at all. I'm simply offering to help."

"Because you keep a hammer in your back pocket?"

"No. But because I know how to do things. Like tracking down and retrieving a stolen Stradivarius that was stuffed into a cabinet with dirty laundry in a second-story flat in Pigalle. Like finding a seventeenth-century Medici artifact that was hidden in the flour tins in an Italian bakery," he said, and she arched an eyebrow as he rattled off some of his jobs. "Like tracking down a Degas drawing that was tucked under a floorboard in a house in Boston."

"And you used your hammer for that?"

His lips curved up in a mild grin. "Yes. I used a hammer for that, and the owner was thrilled to have it back. I can also open most safes."

"Is there anything you can't do?" she asked sarcastically. "Now you're a safecracker, too, MacGyver?"

"I'm not a safecracker," he said as his lips twitched in a grin at the nickname. "But five years in the army working in intelligence gave me a lot of insight about how people think, and the best tools to use to solve problems. And I've been in this line of work long enough to develop some key skills. Those include but are not limited to picking locks, opening safes, removing floorboards quietly, climbing through windows silently, jumping out of windows without a sound. Running across the roof, shimmying down the trellis, then darting through the bushes, and doing it all without being seen."

He left out the part about how a squeaky shoe on the wet cobblestones had gotten him stabbed. Besides, he'd escaped with the prize, despite the squeaky sole.

"My, my," she said, making an *O* with her lips as he tried to sell her on his skills. But he couldn't tell if she was truly impressed or still annoyed. "You dart, you shimmy, you dodge. You are a jack-of-all-trades."

"Why thank you," he said, though he was well aware she was mocking his best sales effort.

"So you want me to be the front woman, sniffing out information, and you can be Captain Adventure?"

"Sure." He managed a smile. "I actually think that's a perfect partnership. One that maximizes what we both bring to the table. Or think of it like this. You're the sniper; I'm the gun."

"But what if I just don't need a gun, Jake? What if all I need are my eyes?" She pointed to her blue eyes. Her gorgeous, pretty-as-a-picture blue eyes that were so damn innocent and sweet-looking, just like the tone she was using now. This woman, she could work him over. He had to stay on his guard.

"Tell you what, Steph. Go to Eli's on Thursday night. If he does have the diamonds in a bowl on his desk, or on the dining room table, or wherever, then all you have to do is stuff those beauties in your pocket and run back to Miami with them. I am happy to call Andrew and say I failed abysmally at my mission."

She didn't answer right away. She simply watched him, like she was studying him. "Hypothetically, if we're partners and I went to his house to scope out the scene, would you wait quietly in a bush or trellis for me? You know, in case there are dangerous guard dogs you need to rescue me from?"

"I doubt you'd need rescuing from anything. But yes, I could do that. And by the way, I know there aren't trellises on your stepfather's property," he said, his voice cool and casual, as he picked up the fork.

"How do you know that?"

"It's my job to know that. His house is on the water. He has palm trees, an orchid tree, a rose bush, an infinity pool, and a boat in a private dock. He lives in a two-story stone house, with a stucco roof, purchased a year ago in a condo development called Corey's Landing."

She raised her eyebrows. The look in her eyes said she was impressed. "You do your homework."

"Maybe I'm not just muscle. Maybe I have the brains, too," he said, tapping his temple. "So what do you say? Are we in? If we find the diamonds, we return them to their rightful owners, the Eli Fund, and presumably that helps your mom, since she helped start the company," he said, then he zeroed in on her soft spot, since it was his, too—looking out for others. "Look, let's say he didn't do it. But someone else did. Let's pretend someone else took something from the fund. What happens if you dig into this and run into this person," he said, and though he was convinced of Eli's guilt, he also knew you could never be too careful, and he couldn't rule out Eli having accomplices he didn't know of yet. "What if you find someone else is involved? I'll be your backup."

"Like a bodyguard?" she asked, a bit playful.

"I give good backup, Steph," he said, and she managed a small smile. "And good protection."

"You know that sounds dirty."

"I know. But I mean it, too. What do you say? You won't rat me out and I won't rat you out, and we help each other get to the bottom of the diamonds." *Stolen diamonds,* he added in his head. He picked up the other fork and handed it to her, wanting her yes. This job would be finished a hell of a lot faster with an inside woman. He held a breath as he waited.

She took the fork but didn't dig into the cake. The fork hovered in midair in her hand. "The diamonds might be in his nightclub."

"They might."

"Eli invited me to go tonight. He won't be there. But they might be in a bank, too. If they're in a bank vault, I doubt your hammer or lock-picking tricks would work."

He nodded. "You're right. And I certainly don't intend to break into a bank. Even I have lines."

"What if they are in a bank?"

"Then I give Andrew that information. He hired me to conduct some recon and drum up intel. If I can nab the diamonds, I certainly will. But if they're guarded in a bank, my job will be of the information-recovery rather than item-recovery nature." He quickly added, "*Our* job."

"Our?" She quirked up the corner of her lips. "So you've already decided we're partners? What if I don't trust you?"

"That doesn't mean we can't be partners. But I also think you probably trust me more than you think. Because you like me," he said with a lopsided grin as he waited patiently for her answer.

She laughed as she shook her head, bemused. Then she roamed her eyes over his face, his chest, his arms. Her gaze wasn't sexual. She seemed to be considering his offer. His plan might be grade-A insane, and Lord only knew that the last time he'd worked with a woman, he'd been burned. But he had no plans of letting her into his heart. Nope. This was only work. Nothing more.

"It seems you have talents that might come in handy," she admitted.

"See? I knew you could be convinced of my talents," he said, wiggling an eyebrow.

She rolled her eyes. "In this case, I was actually thinking of the other talent you mentioned. The one where you could wander around town, ask questions here and there, act like a tourist, and no one thinks anything of it. There are a few things I have in mind. But they require both of us."

He held out his arms wide. "That's what I'm talking about. So does this mean we're working together, Ariel?"

She nodded, then lowered her voice to a whispered warning. "But just work. No funny stuff."

"No funny stuff," he said, agreeing to the necessary rule. Though shucking off the desire he felt for her was no easy task. Hell, it was maddening lust that had raged inside of him when he spotted her on the beach. But that had to end. "I'm not suggesting we fuck. I'm suggesting we track down ten million dollars in stolen diamonds and return them to their rightful owners—the Eli Fund and its middle-America customers. And if we can't do that, we get as much intel on the diamonds as we can. If we work together, we can get the job done faster, cleaner, and be done with each other sooner."

She pointed at him. "Let's start planning now. But nothing else. Got it?"

"You mean, no more rubbing up against my stuffed socks?" he asked drily.

"And no more ripping my clothes off on the beach."

He set down his fork and held out a hand to shake. "Partners."

"Platonic partners," she added.

"Platonic partners," he repeated as they shook across the cake. He could do this. He could absolutely keep his hands off her, no problem. "Let's have some cake and work on our plan. To prove we can just eat cake and work together."

"Instead of trying to gobble each other up?"

"Gobbling? We were gobbling?"

"That's what Marie said it looked like at the Pink Pelican."

He took a forkful of the cake. Soft and spongy and delicious. "Funny. I wouldn't have called it gobbling when I kissed you so hard you melted in my arms."

She rolled her eyes. "What would you have called it?"

He leaned closer and lowered his voice. "Devouring. Kissing you was like a sweet devouring."

CHAPTER FOURTEEN

She'd planned for this contingency.

While Steph was not a clubber, she'd anticipated needing to walk through the doors of Sapphire on this trip. She'd packed accordingly, and the slinky black dress hugged her hips and boosted her breasts, leaving little to the imagination. That was the point of the Little Black Dress in a woman's wardrobe, even though 99 percent of Steph's closet consisted of shorts, bikinis, and tank tops. But the dress helped her to blend in once inside the glittery, sparkling blue club that pulsed with music, liquor, and dark lights.

The beefy security guard lifted the velvet rope for her, ushering her inside.

"Welcome to Sapphire, Ms. Anderson," the guard said.

"Thank you so much."

She'd opted to enter as a VIP. If Eli was offering special treatment, there was no reason not to take it. Jake had made a great point that she couldn't entirely slip through town unknown, so it was better to use her access to her advantage.

Their advantage now.

So weird that last night she'd kissed the man like there was no tomorrow, and tonight they were hands-off partners. After lunch, she'd called Andrew, and he'd confirmed that Jake was his man, so that made her feel better about partnering up with him. Besides, she was pretty sure she needed him, and he'd made a good pitch that they could crack this "case" much faster together. Though she was entering the club solo, she wasn't alone. Jake had arrived earlier, texting her that he was here.

A chestnut-haired beauty with a curvy figure joined Steph at the back door. "I'm Clarissa. I'm the assistant manager. Ferdinand is tied up, but I would love to show you around," the woman said, and she shot a bright, white-toothed smile at Steph. The woman had the skin tone of a local, and Steph briefly rewound to Devon's comments about Eli bringing many jobs to the island. Maybe Clarissa had benefitted from his supposed largesse? A bead of frustration wormed through her. It was irksome that Eli could still manage to do some good, even if he was doing it with someone else's money.

Steph shook Clarissa's hand. "So great to meet you. I'm excited to see the club."

"Let me give you a quick tour, and then we'll make sure you can be up front when Jane performs."

With a hand on her lower back, Clarissa guided Steph through the club. Though it didn't take any special insight to figure out the long mirrored bar was, indeed, the bar, or that the black hardwood floors were, in fact, the dance floor, the VIP treatment was welcome when Clarissa plowed through the crowds on the winding staircase that led to the second level. A balcony wrapped around all four sides of the dance floor up top, giving a perfect view of the crowds below.

Including Jake.

He leaned casually against the bar, a glass of what looked to be Scotch in his hand. No Tommy Bahama shirt tonight. He wore a black T-shirt that showed off his toned, muscular arms and a pair of dark blue jeans. Simple, yet totally hot, even from a distance. She made eye contact, but that was all. That moment was enough for him to walk away from the bar.

On cue.

"Eli loves to watch the crowds from here," Clarissa said, gesturing to the throngs below—young women in tight dresses and guys in shorts and short-sleeve shirts. "You can just feel the energy radiate, can't you?" Clarissa said, inhaling as if she were drawing in that very energy.

"Oh yes, absolutely."

"And," Clarissa continued, pointing a French-manicured nail toward the ceiling, "We have a dozen disco balls. They just make the whole place light up, don't they?"

The silvery disco balls swirled above the floor, casting slivers of rich purple, royal blue, and lush red rays of light on the dance floor. They were retro and seventies, but somehow they weren't cheesy at all. They worked.

"Gorgeous," Steph said, and she meant it.

"Come. Let me show you our VIP rooms," Clarissa said, gesturing to a hallway lined with three paintings—a square, a rectangle, and an oval in black tubular frames that maintained the geometric theme of the art.

"The art is lovely. Anything special to them?" she asked.

"They're from the gallery around the corner. Isla's gallery."

"Ah, but of course." Naturally, Eli would shower his fiancée's business with greenbacks.

Steph peered at the name of the artist in the corner: *Lynx*. So Lynx liked to make shapes, and Eli liked to buy them. The question tugged at her—was the art connected at all to the missing funds? Jake had said they originally thought the fund's missing money had been channeled into art, but now they were sure it had gone into gems. Even so, given Eli's affection for art, she and Jake wanted to know if art played a part.

As a hiding spot.

As they walked down the hallway, the hair on her neck stood on end. She sensed Jake was nearby. That was the plan—as she received the tour, he'd follow behind, peeking into corners, checking out secret passageways, assessing locations for a safe. Steph swallowed nervously. She'd never tried to pull off this sort of cloak-and-dagger routine. But she reminded herself, as Clarissa gave her a tour of the VIP rooms with blue velvet couches and bottle service, that she wasn't the one who had to slink around.

Jake needed to ghost through the club, and he seemed to be doing a damn fine job of it.

He slowed as they passed the three paintings that matched the style he'd seen in the gallery yesterday, though it was hard—no pun intended—to tear his gaze away from Steph's ass. That dress was clinging to her body in all the right places, stirring up not-so-distant memories of how she'd felt in his hands this afternoon on the beach.

The way she'd rubbed against him. How her breath had caught when he'd squeezed those cheeks. Damn. He could use a little breathing room in his jeans right about now.

He zoned in on the art to get his mind away from the off-limits woman who rounded the bend in the hallway, out of sight.

What was the deal with these paintings? They didn't seem very good, but then he knew little about art. He was more interested in what they might be hiding. Most people were creatures of habit. They had their routines, and they followed them, including criminals. Even the smartest of thieves. They might unearth more clever cover-ups and devise trickier schemes, but human nature was human nature, and that didn't change even for the best con men.

That often meant a thief's likes and dislikes were guideposts on the path to cracking a case. Passwords, combinations, and locations were rarely truly cryptic.

Eli liked art.

So Jake needed to study the art. Even if art was no longer the item in question, the art here at the club might tell him something.

As he strolled down the hall, he lightly ran his hand along the frame of the first one, looking for any clues. He didn't expect Eli had hidden a safe right here in plain sight, but something caught his interest. The frame looked awfully heavy for such a light, airy, contemporary piece of art. Didn't modern art have simpler frames? Or no frames at all? But this was a sturdy bastard, and he was damn curious why.

Before he could investigate further, a group of people walked by. He tucked his hands in the pockets of his jeans and struck his best *just-a-guy-wandering-down-the-hall* pose. Seconds later, Steph and Clarissa emerged from a VIP room, their backs to him.

"And here's Eli's office," the woman said, pointing to a door at the end of the hall. "Now, let's get you out to the dance floor. Jane is about to start."

They left his line of sight.

He wandered past Eli's office, contemplating nudging the door open and sniffing around. Then his shoulders tensed, and his spine straightened when someone opened the door.

He caught sight of artwork hanging on the office wall before the man crossed the threshold, his jaw moving back and forth as he crunched loudly. Jake adopted his best *how-did-I-wind-up down-this-hallway* look as he scratched his head.

The big man turned to him and raised an eyebrow. "Can I help you with anything?"

"Just heading back to the dance floor. Looks like it's that way."

The man smiled. There were nuts in his teeth. Cashews, maybe. A snake tattoo curved down his arm. Raising his hand to his lips, he

popped into his mouth a handful of more nuts, presumably, then emitted a low moan of culinary delight as he turned to the office door and
locked it.

Tonight wasn't the best time to scope out that room.

Jake could have left when the tour was over. He could have taken off
after the first song. But the music was lively, the crowd was wild, and
the woman was impossible to look away from.

That was the problem.

A trio of college guys was checking out Steph as she danced near
the small stage, her arms over her head, her hips swaying back and
forth. Her blonde, wavy hair spilled down her spine, and she danced
like she was one with her body, like he imagined she moved underwater.
Graceful, effortless, natural.

He stood watch by the edge of the dance floor, the darkness of
the purple lights from overhead eclipsing him. He alternated between
keeping an eye on her and not letting the guys out of sight. Didn't like
them. Before Steph had arrived, he'd spotted them at the end of the
bar, and he swore the blond dude with the stupid-ass grin had dropped
something in a drink. Jake had no clue what had become of the drink,
but he was going to make damn sure the guy didn't try to pull that shit
with Steph or anyone else.

She was smart, and he doubted she'd take a drink from a stranger,
but when the guy inched closer to her, a glass of clear liquid in his hand,
Jake wasn't going to take a chance.

The blond dude smiled and said hello to her.

Oh hell no. That was not going to fly.

Quickly threading through the packed crowd on the dance floor,
he found his way to her and dropped a hand on her hip. She flinched
at first, then glanced back at him.

"Oh. Didn't realize you were still here," she said.

"Still here," he said, meeting her blue-eyed gaze. They hadn't talked after their recon mission—she'd gone straight to the stage, and he didn't want to spend too much time with her in public, though a few minutes now, by the darkened edge of the stage, amid the huge crowd, was safe enough. Jake's eyes drifted briefly to the blond guy who hadn't quite gotten the message. He was standing far too close, so Jake tugged her near him. "A woman like you doesn't need a frat boy," he said in a low voice, just for her.

She arched an eyebrow. "Is that so? What does a woman like me need?"

The guy flubbed his lips and walked away. Mission accomplished. Jake could walk away, too.

But he didn't. He was mere millimeters from her, and that coconut scent was in his damn nostrils again. Reminding him of how her skin tasted. How she smelled when he'd kissed her. And how goddamn much he wanted to wrap her legs around his waist.

Digging his thumb into her hip, he answered her. "Someone who knows how to savor a stunning marine biologist."

That earned him a sparkling smile. She raised her chin as the music pulsed from the stage. "Savoring is your specialty, I take it?"

While he hadn't cut across the floor to flirt, he found himself unable to stop. Being this close to her short-circuited all his brain cells. "Oh, believe you me. I am excellent at that pursuit," he said, letting go of her hip, so his fingers drifted across the fabric of her dress to her belly.

"How would you do that? Savor me, that is."

He flicked her belly button ring through the material, and her breath caught in response. "I'd run my tongue across this ring, then properly kiss you all over. Every inch. That's what you need. That's what you deserve."

"Proper kissing? Everywhere?" she asked, her voice breathy and low, but he heard every word because they were only for him.

He splayed his palm over her flat belly. The club goers crowded them in, crushing them closer together, and the press of bodies and the tightness of the space made it so hardly anyone could tell who was with whom. "Everywhere," he said as his thumb dropped lower, tracing a line along the waistband of her panties, making his intentions clear. "Everywhere along your beautiful body."

She shivered, and her lips parted, but she said nothing. Maybe she was wondering why the hell he was saying these things when they'd agreed to cool it. Hell, he was wondering, too. "You deserve someone who craves the taste of your lips. The feel of your body. Most of all, a woman like you deserves a man who understands the three-to-one ratio."

She scrunched her brows together. "What's that?"

He brushed her blonde strands away from her ear, cupped a hand over it, and whispered, "I would make sure you come three times before I even do once."

She gasped, and her lips fell open.

He wrenched back. "I'll pick you up tomorrow at two. I'd better go before someone sees how much I want you right now."

Because he wasn't supposed to. He wasn't supposed to want her this badly.

He made his way to the exit. The same guy from last night was manning it. Jake cleared his throat. "I believe there's a gentleman in there who might be slipping something into women's drinks," he said, then described the blond guy.

Cal Winters nodded a thanks. "I'll take care of it right away."

Then Jake returned to his hotel room and pictured working on that three-to-one ratio.

CHAPTER FIFTEEN

Shorts and T-shirt, skirt and tank top, or sundress? What on earth do you wear to a . . . stakeout?

Was this even a stakeout?

Steph shook her head, answering her own question.

No. It was more of a mission. An intel-gathering mission, to be precise. And her role was playing the getaway driver as well as the diamond babysitter.

Still, she couldn't decide what to wear. Her bed was a mess, littered with clothes and bikinis, because one should always have a bikini handy in a beach town. She grabbed the pink one with polka dots, tugged it on, pulled on a sundress, and slid into flip-flops. There. Seemed a suitable wardrobe for this next phase of the plan.

She was grabbing her purse when someone rapped on the door.

She froze.

She'd hoped to be in the lobby at two and meet him there. Because Jake in her room? That would test all her sweet-devouring, three-to-one, do-bad-things-to-me resolve.

You totally did not fantasize about him last night. You were not think-ing of him whatsoever and the way his fingers danced across the outline of your panties on the dance floor.

Another knock.

She smoothed a hand over her dress. She was steel. She could so do this.

She opened the door, and her willpower was ready to wave the white flag. Even in the cheesy palm-tree button-down shirt and touristy hat with the slogan It's Better in the Caymans, the man was just too good-looking to be real. Starting with those arms. So firm and strong, they were the image of temptation. She suspected they'd feel good to touch as he moved over her.

There it went—another roller-coaster dive of butterflies inside her.

And that chest. Broad and sturdy. She pictured her hands spread across his pecs.

Then, those eyes. Those see-into-my-soul green eyes that crinkled at the corners.

But most of all, her gaze lingered on his lips. She was already acquainted with their talents. She could only imagine what else they could do.

"Let me just grab the stone," she said, and started to close the door and leave him in the hallway before she combusted from staring at him.

He stuck his foot in the door. "I'll join you."

She waved him off. "That's OK. I'll be super fast."

He flashed her a dirty grin. "I want to prove I can keep my hands to myself. Just like I did last night."

She narrowed her eyes. "I seem to recall your hands were on me. But by all means, show me your willpower," she said, opening the door, because now he was testing her resolve and she wasn't one to back down from a challenge.

"I thought you might enjoy seeing that feat of strength from me," he said with a wink, reminding her of why she'd liked him so damn much the first night. The man was charming.

And . . . the man also thought her stepfather was a criminal.

"Nice costume," she said, reminding herself to keep the conversation light between them. To avoid the dicier topics of guilt or innocence, as well as the more dangerous matters of lust.

He gestured to his getup. "I know you're a big fan of the way I look in Hawaiian shirts."

"You are definitely one hundred percent pure tourist," she said, and shut the door behind her, then pointed to the small room. Best to be completely casual and friendly with Jake, nothing more. "It's not the fanciest hotel on the island, but it's home sweet home for now," she joked, as if a hotel room would reveal details of who she was. But it did, in a way. The beige tile floor was littered with her tour supplies—snorkels she'd picked up earlier in the day and mesh bags full of underwater masks, as well as climbing gear. The nightstand boasted a paperback she'd been reading—a true-life adventure of a man who'd hiked across China, as well as her e-reader for when she needed something saucier.

Meanwhile, her assortment of bikinis and clothes was strewn across her bed.

"You could start a bathing suit shop," he remarked.

"I'm considering buying stock in bikinis."

"It's like an explosion. Or maybe they multiplied."

"I couldn't decide what to—" Then she stopped and clasped her hand over her mouth. His green gaze shifted from the bed to her.

"What to wear this afternoon?" he supplied, but his tone wasn't jokey or sarcastic. It was soft and vulnerable. The look in his eyes was, too. As if he wanted her to say yes. The way he gazed at her made her want to say yes to so much more. To whatever he'd ask.

Oh Lord, this was so much tougher than she'd expected.

She nodded and breathed a quiet, "Yes."

He stepped closer. Raised his hand. Traced an invisible line in the air, inches from her, traveling from her shoulder, along her breasts, down her belly, to her hip. She swallowed and breathed out hard as hot shivers followed his hand. He wasn't even touching her, but the sensations, the mere possibilities, ignited her.

This was precisely why she didn't want him in her room.

This was precisely why she wanted him in her room.

She was torn, her body asking for one thing, her mind telling her to just focus on the job because she and Jake were at odds.

"The outfit you chose is perfect," he said, his voice low and gravelly, and so damn sexy that it nearly sapped all that remaining resistance. Especially when his fingertips brushed against her waist.

Somehow, she uttered a thanks, then made her way to the safe. She began to press the buttons on the lock. In an instant he was behind her, his hand on her hand, his chest against her back. Her mind returned to the flash of images that had played before her closed lids last night in her room as she satisfied that sweet ache he'd left her with on the dance floor. That same damn ache camped out again, beating a pulse in her belly, asking her to move closer to him. There. Right there. So she was aligned with the length of his strong, sturdy body.

He wrapped his fingers over hers.

"What are you doing?" She wasn't sure if the question was about the safe or his intentions. Though his hard body—hard everywhere she wanted him to be—made it clear his intentions lived in the same vicinity as hers.

He drew a breath, then brushed his lips on her shoulder. She was ready to turn around, grab him, pull him to her bed, and let him strip her to nothing and take her. It had been a long time. So damn long that her body was ready to defect from her brain, which was trying to tell her she didn't trust men as far as she could throw them and this man was nothing but red flags.

He whispered a combination of numbers. Five of them, to be precise.

The hair on her neck stood on end, and she froze.

She unfroze as he pushed those numbers on her safe, and the door popped open. She swiveled around and pressed her hands on his chest. She stared at him like he'd just crash-landed in her room on a rocket ship. "How did you do that?"

He shrugged and shot her a smile that could melt panties. "Told you I could open safes. I just wanted to show you." He brushed a strand of hair off her shoulder. "So you know I'm a good partner."

He bent his head closer to her neck once more and dusted another soft, barely there, almost chaste kiss on her. She pressed her hand to his chest, undeterred. "But *how* did you do that?" she asked again, refusing to focus on that kiss.

"Ariel," he said casually. "Two, seven, four, three, five."

Her jaw dropped, then she swatted him. "Not. Fair. You tricked me again."

He laughed deeply, the booming sound carrying across the room. She nudged him away from the safe and grabbed the box with the diamond her stepfather had given her. A dose of embarrassment surged through her.

"C'mon, Steph," he said, reaching for her.

She shrugged him off. "C'mon what?"

"I was just trying to show you what I could do."

"Yeah, and you sure did. You made me look stupid for picking that as my combination."

"I'm sure it's not your ATM pin, though," he said matter-of-factly, his sunshine eyes lighting up.

"No. It's not," she said, patting herself mentally on the back for choosing a slightly more complicated string for her bank. "I just can't believe I picked something you figured out in two seconds."

"It's a name you like. It's your nickname. Don't feel bad. People usually choose familiar words for their combinations. Understanding habits and human nature is part of my job."

"But you were kissing me and trying to make me melt in your arms to give it up."

He laughed once more and shook his head. "Nope. You're wrong there. You didn't give it up. And I was just kissing your neck because you smelled so damn good I couldn't help myself." He held up his hands in surrender. "Twenty-four hours and I've already broken the rules. I promise it won't happen again, and please do forgive me for not being able to resist you in that moment when you looked so ridiculously hot in front of the safe."

He doffed an imaginary top hat, like a Victorian-era gentleman apologizing properly.

She huffed, wishing she could stay mad at him. She clutched the box to her chest. "Fine. Apology accepted. Now let's go before you feel compelled to toss me on the bed and do very bad things to me as you practice ratios."

He groaned, a deep, throaty sound that told her she'd regained the upper hand.

Momentarily.

As she drove to the diamond district with him, she gripped the steering wheel of her rental so she wouldn't be tempted to run a hand along his arm. "OK, let's review the plan. You're going to get as many details on my diamond as you possibly can so we can try to figure out where it came from," she said, her heart pinching with the hope that his intel would somehow make it clear that her rock was a simple gift from Eli.

"Yep. And what it's worth, of course. To see if it could even add up. See, Andrew and I were originally thinking Eli might have moved the stolen money in art, like we talked about," Jake said, and she winced at the word *stolen*. "But moving that much in art is conspicuous. It's much easier to get on a plane with a handful of diamonds than with big wads of cash or hundreds of canvases. Shipping art that expensive, too, would be noticed, with the insurance a thief would need to cover it."

Another wince. Another cringe. She wished he'd stop using those damn words.

"But gems," Jake said, continuing his theorizing, "Eli can put on a string and wear that around his neck on the flight. He can have his fiancée wear them. Doesn't matter. Once they're diamonds, they travel easily on your person."

"You don't know he transported them on his neck, Jake," she said through tight lips, keeping her eyes on the road. "We don't know that he transported them at all."

"Right," he said, as if the word had ten syllables. "Maybe he had a private jet. But even so, you have to go through customs, and let's say, hypothetically, if *someone* were to transport diamonds, or sapphires, or rubies, they're movable much easier than a ton of art. That's why a smart guy like—" he said, then stopped himself. "A smart person would take the stolen money and put it into jewels. Especially if someone can help him with *safe* transport."

She knew he was referencing that e-mail, that damn incriminating e-mail, and all those other documents, too. She didn't want to think about those details right now. She shifted to the strategy for today.

"So is there a secret back exit at International Diamonds? You'd better not sneak out the back door with my gem," she said, zoning in on the task at hand—to find out how valuable these stones were.

"I promise I'm not going to dart through the diamond merchant's shop to make off with your rock."

"How do I know?" she asked, since it was, admittedly, risky to hand over the diamond for a few minutes. But it was riskier for her to go into the shop herself.

He rustled around in the passenger seat. At the red light, she glanced over. He was digging into his back pocket. He extracted his wallet and flipped it open, tapping the plastic covering his driver's license. "Here you go. Take it. My identification. Can't get anywhere without it. Plus, you've got all my credit cards in there, too, so you can have a spending spree if I turn out to be some crazy escape artist taking off with your diamond."

He set the wallet in the center console, and her lips twitched up in a grin. "That's a reasonable form of collateral."

The light changed, and she pressed the gas, weaving through the afternoon traffic. "What happens if someone sees us together? What do I say? Who are you?"

He flashed a lopsided grin. "Well, you'll be waiting in the car, so no one will. But if someone does, that's easy. I'm a customer of Ariel's Island Eco-Adventure Tours, and you hit on me on your dive tour."

She rolled her eyes. "As if I would do that."

"You totally hit on me. You couldn't resist. I was underwater in my swim trunks, and you couldn't stop staring, so you hit on me," he said, the cocky bastard, as he dropped his hand onto her bare thigh. She hitched in a breath.

"You wish," she said, trying to ignore the fact that she liked his hand on her leg.

"It's true. I speak the full truth," he said as he tugged the ball cap lower on his head. "You picked me up and you insisted on having me."

"Just like you insisted on kissing me back in my hotel room," she said as she flicked on her blinker and turned onto Wayboard Street.

"I'll try to do a better job resisting you," he said, but as she locked eyes with him, the look in his said resistance would be tough.

She nearly swerved when a car honked its horn at her.

Better pay attention to the road than his sexy eyes.

CHAPTER SIXTEEN

International Diamonds commanded the corner of the street. The sign above the shop glittered, with huge cutout gems bookending the name.

He pushed open the door, and a blast of cool air-conditioning greeted him. He was nearly blinded by the dazzling displays of gems. Cases upon cases. Row upon row. Necklaces, and bracelets, and rings, and watches, and even barrettes.

The shop was busy, thronging with curious tourists, judging from the attire. But also a few businessmen, he reasoned, when he spotted a pair of men in slacks and button-down shirts at the far counter. They were engaged in what looked to be a deep discussion with an employee. This was good. The busier the shop was, the less likely anyone would remember him, even though the diamond he had was memorable.

He wandered along the counters, peering through the glass at the loose gems, absently drumming his fingers along the case.

"May I help you, sir?"

The question came from a young woman in a white lab coat. She wore black glasses and had her dark hair twisted up in a bun.

"That'd be great," he said, reaching into his pocket to remove the gem. "My sister's husband gave her a diamond to try to win her back after he broke her heart. But he did it again, and we're just trying to figure out how much this pretty little number is worth, even though nothing's worth the cost of the heartache he gave her."

The woman shot him a sympathetic smile. "I'm so sorry to hear that. Diamonds are a wonderful gift, but so much more wonderful when it's a true expression of love."

"Couldn't agree more. And she just wants to donate the money to charity now. She doesn't plan on keeping it. She wants something good to come of that bastard's cheating ways."

"I completely understand. Let's see what you have," she said, spreading out a velvet cloth on the counter. Jake laid the diamond on it.

"Oh my," the woman said under her breath. She looked up at Jake. "He really did mess up."

Jake laughed lightly. "He sure did."

Using a tweezers-like object, the woman carefully plucked the diamond from the cloth, raised it to her face, then peered at it through a small magnifying glass. "This is gorgeous," she said as she regarded the stone.

Jake waited as she considered it from all angles.

Once she set it down, she fixed on a closed smile, then spoke in a crisp tone. "This is watermarked."

A bolt of nerves crashed into him. Shit. Watermarked had to be bad. Was that like trying to use counterfeit money? Was she going to press a button behind the counter, shutter the metal blinds, and set off alarms to keep him caged in?

"Is that so?" he asked, keeping his tone as even as it could be. "Where does it come from?"

"Not all diamonds are watermarked. But some are, and a watermarked diamond means it comes from a particular mine. This is from the Frayer mine in the Northwest Territories in Canada, which specializes in conflict-free, politically correct diamonds mined from the subarctic north."

Jake nodded and released his breath. Whew. "Well, at least the ex has that point in his favor," he said, though his mind leaped several steps ahead to Eli "The Thief" Thompson. Was he a thief with a politically correct conscience?

"Yes, this is one of the best-regarded diamond mines in the entire world. And these diamonds with the blue tint are highly valuable. At this size and carat, I would estimate this is worth at least ten thousand dollars."

He nearly bit his tongue, holding in the whoop of both shock and triumph he was tempted to unleash as the amount registered, and he added up numbers. "That so?"

"It is indeed," she said, her dark eyes fixed on him, as if she were studying him. "I can handle the transaction for you if you'd like. We have handled a few of these diamonds recently. Every time we receive a new one, we can easily find buyers all over the world. I can give you full value today, sir. Are you ready to get started?" she asked, sounding way more eager than he'd expected for someone forking over cash, rather than being on the receiving end. Her gaze remained locked on his, and her stare was intense.

And, admittedly, a little odd. Like she was ready to pounce on him if he said yes.

"Let me talk to my sister, and we'll be back tomorrow."

"Excellent. I look forward to seeing you. I'm Monica. You can ask for me. I'll be looking forward to helping you."

He saluted her as he pocketed the gem with his other hand. "Great talking to you, Monica."

Two minutes later, he climbed inside Steph's Jeep and handed her the five-figure gem. "Your stepdad is generous. That bad boy is worth ten K. You're going to change the combination on your safe tonight, Ariel."

Her eyes widened to the size of moons. "Are you kidding me?"

He shook his head. "I assure you I'm not," he said, then told her the details of the mine as they stayed parked on the side of the road, the afternoon sun shining through the window. "So Eli gets them from this Canadian mine, from a merchant who sources from there, probably through Constantine Trevino. That's the guy he was in contact with back when he was still at the fund. He gets all the diamonds while he's still in the United States working with this guy," he said, though the part that worried Jake was what Eli was doing with the stones now that he was here in the land of do-whatever-you-want-with-money. Was he selling them all off and converting them back into cash? Was he selling them in small chunks? Wilder had said someone had brought a small batch of these blue diamonds into International Diamonds recently. Did that mean Eli had already turned a few stones into greenbacks?

Jake doubted it. Eli was cunning. He was probably cashing them in bit by bit, stone by stone, so as not to draw undue attention. Time was of the essence.

Later today, he'd call Andrew and update him on this latest discovery. See if his client had any new intel on those e-mails he was trying to decode. Especially given that the diamonds were watermarked, Jake had no interest in hunting diamonds that were highly traceable. He needed to know that point A led to point B—that the stolen money was used to buy the gems from that mine. The clues added up, but facts were awfully nice, too.

"Once he gets the diamonds from that mine, all he has to do is get on a plane to the Caymans with a pocketful of diamonds," Jake added.

Steph arched an eyebrow. "A pocketful? I don't know. Maybe he doesn't have as many as you think. Maybe he's giving them away as gifts. For his fiancée, for me. We have no idea how many he actually has," she said, her voice rising as she once again tried to poke holes in the possibility of what her stepfather had done.

It was noble, and sweet, in a way, that she wanted to believe the guy. But she was also dead wrong.

"I guarantee he has more than a few. A lot more. In fact, I know exactly how many he has," Jake said, his lips twitching in a confident grin.

She knit her brow together as she cranked the AC button, since the car was heating up. "How do you know?"

"Because it adds up," he said, tapping his temple. "Math."

"OK, Mr. Math. Tell me how two plus two equals *a lot more*."

"The e-mail from the merchant. It said *safe transport for a grand*."

Her jaw went slack. "Seriously?"

He nodded. "Two plus two," he said, his tone gentler, even though excitement was coursing through him as he worked with her to assemble clues. He'd nearly forgotten how fun it could be, now and then, to work in tandem.

She shook her head, a flicker of sadness in her eyes as she spoke. "It does add up. Ten million divided by ten thousand is indeed one thousand," she said, her tone heavy, as she divided the missing money by the cost of one stone. "Otherwise known as *a grand*."

Safe transport for a grand.

"It seems the safe transport reference wasn't about the cost of the transport, but *how many* they were making plans to move," Jake said.

She ran a hand through her hair and sighed. "I just wish—"

Her eyes snapped away from his. She pointed and slid down in the driver's seat. He glanced around. A man with salt-and-pepper hair headed down the block.

"What's wrong?"

"Tristan," she whispered like a hiss, then peered out the window. "Shit."

In a blur, she unbuckled her seat belt, slid out of the seat, and climbed on top of him. "Kiss me so he doesn't notice me."

No time to think. Just follow orders. Ex-military, Jake knew how to do that, and this was the easiest order ever. He cupped her face and sealed his mouth to hers. He looped his hands in her hair and swept his tongue across the seam of her mouth. She moaned quietly and parted her lips for him.

To hide her more, he grabbed the ball cap from his head, gathered her long blonde hair in his hand, and covered it up with the hat on her head. He could feel her smile as he tucked her hair into the cap while barely breaking the kiss.

"Thank you," she murmured, then returned her mouth to his.

He was positive the dude had walked past them now. But hell if he was going to stop. Not as she straddled him, angling her body in a perfect position for fucking. Not as she started to slowly rock her hips into him. And not as she kissed back harder and hungrier, her lips greedy for all this contact. She tasted like tropical temptation itself. He explored her mouth thoroughly, tangoing his tongue with hers, tasting her lips, devouring her.

He couldn't even remember why they'd decided on no funny stuff. This was worth it.

She picked up speed and started riding him harder. As her breaths grew faster, he half wondered if she was going to bring herself to orgasm by humping his erection in his shorts. While he loved that idea and wanted nothing more than to hear her little moans turn into full-blown cries of pleasure, he also didn't want the two of them to get arrested for public fornication.

Opening one eye as she kissed him, he scanned the street. Coast was clear.

Gently, he pushed her off him. But this was not going to be the end. "I'm driving," he said. "And I'm finishing what you just started. If that's a problem, you need to tell me now."

"It's not a problem," she whispered, and the look in her eyes was full of lust, and said yes.

He turned on the engine and drove away from the diamond district. Five minutes later, he pulled into a parking garage in a nearby shopping center and found the quietest floor. He grabbed a spot next to the wall and pulled her into the backseat.

"So much for no funny stuff," he said, sliding her sexy body alongside his. Right now, he didn't care about rules. He was driven with need for her.

"You mean this won't make me laugh?"

"If I'm doing it right, you won't be chuckling at all. You'll be screaming my name," he said, running his fingertip along her mouth as he tugged her next to him. His hand traveled along the bare skin of her legs. So damn soft. As she stretched out beside him, her eyes locked with his. The look in hers was vulnerable and hungry at the same time. She wanted this and she wanted to give her body to him.

"Make me . . . ," she whispered, taking a beat, "scream your name."

She parted her thighs.

Killing any more resolve he had.

Not that he had much. It vanished when she'd jumped him on the street minutes ago. Now, it was far in the rearview mirror as he brushed the inside of her thigh. She quivered in his arms, and her reaction sent the temperature inside him soaring.

"Challenge accepted," he said, and she smiled in that sexy-sweet way she had, then her eyes floated closed as he reached the damp panel of her bikini bottoms. He inhaled sharply as he brushed his index finger across that lovely wetness. His dick twitched against his shorts, wanting to find a temporary home inside her. He was so damn eager to bury himself inside her, to slide into her, to make her back arch and her toes curl as he took her to the edge.

But this moment wasn't about him getting off. He wanted to watch her writhe in pleasure. To hear her cries. To see her lips form his name as she came undone. He slid a finger across her, gliding over her slick heat. Oh hell, she felt fucking fantastic, and lust crashed into all corners of his body as she shuddered and rocked into his hand.

He dropped his mouth to hers, claiming her lips in a hot kiss as he tugged her bikini lower, then returned to all that fantastic wetness that coated his fingers. She rocked into him as he stroked her and kissed her, and whatever resistance she'd had seemed so far gone, too.

∾⤳

She was supposed to be denying this.

She was supposed to be stronger.

But she wanted to forget what she'd just learned. She wanted a break from all this thinking about good guys and bad guys, cons and crimes. She wanted to turn off her mind and let her body take over.

Because this man knew what to do with her. Those talented fingers. That wicked mouth. He kissed like he was the reigning world champion in the sport of kissing, and she was his perfect partner. His lips were a dream, and his mouth tasted fantastic, and now he was touching her right where she wanted him.

He stroked faster, hitting her in all the right spots. She raised her hips, meeting his hand, needing his fingers. Craving so much more. Sparks raced through her bloodstream with every move he made, and soon she couldn't concentrate on kissing him. She could only narrow in on the agonizingly exquisite ache between her legs.

"God, it feels so good, Jake."

He thrust his fingers into her, sending her hips shooting up. "You're so sexy all the time, but like this, when you're all turned on, you're out of this world," he whispered in her ear, his voice low and dirty, the words heating her up even more.

"I thought about you last night," she said, her breathing turning erratic. Hot, quick pulses spread through her with every touch, every stroke.

"Yeah? When you were all alone on that hotel bed, you were getting off to me?" he asked as he crooked a finger inside her, and she gasped, crying out loudly in pleasure. Wild sensations burst through her body in quick waves as he fucked her with his fingers, thrusting inside her, rubbing that swollen bundle of nerves where she ached for him. Fireworks popped in her brain. Bright colors flashed before her eyelids.

"You got me all worked up on the dance floor. You were all I pictured as I touched myself," she said as the sensations whipped faster through her and wild sparks rained down on her.

"Was I doing this?" he asked as his fingers rained pleasure down on her. "Or was I fucking you? Was I taking you deep, bent over the bed, you screaming out in pleasure?"

A flip switched with his dirty words. His sexy, filthy words. No one had ever talked to her like this. It was addictive. It was orgasmic. Her belly tightened, and her climax crested into view.

She cried out as she rocked into his hand, hips bucking wildly, pleasure radiating through her. She grabbed his hair, clutched his skull, and pulled him back to her lips as she rode his hand shamelessly in the backseat of her car in the corner of a parking garage in the Caymans.

Coming undone.

Once the orgasm ebbed away, she brushed her palm along his hard-on. "Mmmm," she murmured. "Let me take care of you."

He didn't have the chance to respond, because a car drove by, then another. Back to reality. Their momentary escape into a quiet parking garage bubble had ended.

"Don't think for a second I don't want that. But you need to know I'm also completely satisfied having made you feel good."

The man was a giver.

Kill me now.

CHAPTER SEVENTEEN

Before the sun even cracked through his window, his phone rang with the *Mission: Impossible* theme song.

He blinked, grabbed it, and answered the call. "Hey, Andrew."

"I've got more details," his client said, and Jake could practically hear the man bouncing on the other end of the line. He didn't know Andrew well, but he was willing to bet the man was on the deck of his Miami home, watching the sun peek above the horizon, some sort of excitement in his step.

"Tell me," Jake said, his voice still gravelly with sleep. He'd called Andrew last night and given him the latest report.

"My IT team was able to decipher a few more e-mails. And one of them specifically references a deal with the Frayer mine."

Jake sat up straight in bed and pumped a fist. "Excellent!"

That was the sort of info that made his mission airtight. Exactly how he needed it to be as he zeroed in on the prize.

Jewels.

And jewels equaled his payday, and his payday meant college for the kids.

He talked more with Andrew, then he swung his feet to the floor and headed for the shower, ready to tackle the day with a laser focus.

❦

The sun glared at her. Shining brightly. Mocking her.

She sat up in bed, rubbed her eyes, and tossed off the sheets. She made her way to the bathroom and brushed her teeth, staring at her reflection in the mirror.

She swore there was a devil on one shoulder, an angel on the other.

You caved.

But it felt so good.

You don't trust men. Men are trouble.

Hello? Who said anything about trust? We were discussing orgasms.

You are supposed to focus on business. On your own business. On your stepdad's business. Not that hot-as-sin man's business.

But I didn't even get down to business with him the way I wanted, so back off, Angel.

She spat out the toothpaste, rinsed her mouth, and stretched her arms.

She left the bathroom, wandered to the safe, and tapped in her new combination. H-A-P-P-Y-T-U-R-T-L-E. The door popped open, and her diamond was safe and sound with the new combo. Even if they never found more or uncovered any other details, at least she had a jewel that she could turn into cash, and use it as a gift for her mother.

True, it didn't come close to covering the original investment her mother made in the business, nor the missing money, but ten thousand dollars was nothing to scoff at. Convincing her mother to take the money from the diamond was entirely another matter. But Steph would cross that bridge when she came to it. For now, she grabbed her phone and headed to her tiny balcony. The sliding glass door squeaked as she opened it. She held a hand over her eyes as she soaked in the most beautiful sight in the world. Even from her less-than-world-class accommodations, she still had a view of the crystal-blue ocean and the endless sky.

She inhaled.

Drew the natural beauty into her lungs, letting it feed her, fuel her. All that blue, from the gentle waves in the water up to the clear sky. The very definition of happiness. She closed her eyes briefly, enjoying the warmth on her skin.

When she opened her eyes, she zeroed in on business. She clicked the screen on her phone and spotted an e-mail from her brother.

> The video is up and running. I imagine you'll
> be inundated with dive requests now. Love ya,
> miss ya, stay out of trouble.

She scrolled through the rest of her messages and nearly clapped with glee because the video ad he'd made was working already. She had two new inquiries for scuba tours. From her post on the balcony, she responded immediately, crossing her fingers that the inquiries would turn into tours. That this was happening. Her business was growing stronger, and she had her mom to thank for it. The woman had rescued her business from the pit of despair.

She dialed her favorite person.

"Namaste, my love."

Steph laughed. "You're such a yoga dork."

"And a happy downward-facing dog to you, too. How are you? How is everything going in the Caribbean?"

"It's great. Prepping for my tours and just seeing some old friends," she said, thinking *Devon and Sandy qualified, right?*, even though she'd been mostly busy with Jake and snooping on her stepdad. "And I saw Eli, too. Haven't pilfered his watch yet, but he does have a swank Rolex."

Her mother hissed. "Bastard. Lying, scheming, cheating, Rolex-wearing bastard." Her mom sighed heavily. "Shame on me. I think I just earned myself ten points of bad karma. I need to go apologize to the universe for that verbal tic I just unleashed. How is the dear?"

Steph flashed back to her brunch with Eli, cycling through terms to describe the man—*chipper, upbeat, happy*. Instead, she went with: "He's his usual self. The weird thing was he mentioned something about focusing on his charitable endeavors these days. I never knew he was a big charity guy."

Her mother scoffed. "Ha. He was hardly a big charitable supporter. Getting money out of him was like bleeding a rock."

"You mean, you don't know how to bleed a rock, Mom? If you'd just asked me I would tell you," Steph joked.

"See? If I'd only thought to ask you. I need to skedaddle, darling. I'm trying to catch a morning yoga class. Your friend Lance is going with me."

Steph tilted her head. She hadn't known Lance to do yoga. "Lance? My boat guy Lance?"

"Yes. He's quite flexible."

"Mom!" Steph admonished.

"I don't mean like that. I mean, he's quite flexible in his cat and cow and warrior poses. You just assumed I meant something dirty. Speaking of dirty, have you followed my advice? Found a hot sexy guy for a little something?"

Butterflies swooped through her belly as she returned to Jake. To his hands, and his mouth, and his sexy, sinful side. "As a matter of fact, I did," she said, though yesterday was a one-time lapse, and she could not, would not go there again. "But it won't be a regular thing."

"Why not? What's he like?"

"He's funny, and rugged, and smart. Smoking hot, too."

"Sounds perfect for an island tryst."

Island tryst.

She liked the sound of that. In theory. In practice, it was fraught with too much danger. Not only for her heart, but for her life. Jake was hot and funny and wickedly talented, but they didn't see eye to eye. They were coming at the diamonds from opposite angles.

The evidence was mounting that Eli indeed had a stash of diamonds. But Steph wanted to get to the truth of the diamonds and convince Eli to return them. Jake wanted justice, too, but he also wanted Eli's head.

There was no way an island tryst could work.

After she finished the call, she dropped the name of the diamond mine into the search bar on her phone. She read about its commitment to politically correct mining, its adherence to world standards on labor, and the fact that half of its proceeds went to schools in Africa.

Could this be one of Eli's new charitable endeavors? The website listed some of its biggest supporters for its charitable arm and she studied the names closely.

"Ha!" she declared out loud. Her stepdad's name was nowhere to be seen.

But another name caught her attention.

Isla Evans.

His fiancée.

⁓

Jake waited for Eli.

Because work was all that mattered, he tackled it with determined vigor and blinders on.

At 9:22 a.m., Eli opened the front door, shut it behind him, and walked down the stone path toward his circular driveway. In his right hand, he tossed his car keys up and down a few inches, like he'd done the other day.

He also stopped to sniff the orchids and the roses.

The man was a creature of habit, which boded well for Jake. Men who followed routines were easiest to track. Eli seemed to have his, except . . .

One thing was different this time.

Today, he didn't waft the scent of roses into his nostrils with his free hand. Eli's left hand was tucked inside his pants pocket the whole time. Grabbing binoculars, Jake peered through the lenses to see if he could figure out what the man was up to. He zeroed in on the pocket, and judging from the outline of Eli's hand, it sure looked like he was clutching something in that pocket.

Not that.

But something else precious. Maybe a small pouch with jewels? He was willing to bet that Eli had diamonds from the Frayer mine in his pocket this morning.

After Eli got into his car, Jake followed him, keeping his eye on the target with a new intensity, zoning in on the reason he was in the Cayman Islands in the first place. For a job. And that job meant he needed to know the target and avoid distractions.

Like sexy, feisty, fantastic women. Like one in particular who felt like magic in his hands.

He'd failed miserably yesterday at avoiding distractions. The memory of Steph coming undone in the backseat of her car threatened to derail him again today. Her cries of pleasure echoed in his mind, turning him on again.

He gripped the steering wheel, frustration searing through him. Why had he thought he could pull off a tryst with Steph Anderson? The woman was right to have tried to put her foot down when they'd teamed up, but then she'd gone and kissed him in her car. A kiss that turned into a hell of a lot more in the parking garage.

His jaw clenched as he focused on the road. Foot on gas. Hands on wheel. Eyes on concrete.

Then his dick had the audacity to announce its intentions to have her again. Fucking traitorous prick.

Settle down, boy. We need to focus.

Jake did not need to be having dirty thoughts as he followed her stepfather. He repeated that word. *Stepfather.* He was crossing his lines and breaking his rules, because Jake Harlowe did not get involved on a job. Been there, done that, had the scars to prove it didn't work.

He narrowed in on Eli's car, parking outside the Royal Bank of the Caymans. Would it be a short trip or a longer one this time? Jake pulled over, too, watching Eli from behind his sunglasses as the man hopped out of his car and sauntered into the bank. Jake kept a reasonable distance and followed him inside this time.

A marble floor greeted visitors, and cool, perfectly modulated air pumped through the lobby. Tellers tended to customers behind tall oak counters, while bankers parked at desks worked on more complicated transactions. Eli ignored all of them, striding toward the back, where a man in a pinstriped suit greeted him and held out a hand to shake. The suited man opened the door, and Eli followed him through. Jake wandered casually in that direction, but a guard stood watch.

Staring intently in the distance.

Jake patted his pockets and took a gamble. "Ah hell," he mumbled.

The guard looked up. "Can I help you with something, sir?"

"Crap. I wish. Unless you've got the spare key to my safe deposit box back there?" he asked in a lighthearted voice, pointing in the direction Eli had gone.

The guard smiled faintly. "No, sir."

"I'll be back, then. Must have left it on the darn counter. Need to get my baseball cards."

"See you when you return."

As Jake left the bank, he added up the details in his head. There was no definitive proof that Eli was adding gems to a stash in his safe deposit in the bank, or trading more in. There wasn't proof of anything yet. But there was quite a bit of circumstantial evidence that Eli kept at least some jewels in his house. Seemed Steph had been right on that count with her first gut instinct that the gems were in his home.

Good thing he was working with the inside woman.

Working.

He repeated that word as he returned to his car.

Working. That's what he was doing. Working. Not dreaming up new ways to make her cry out in pleasure.

Jake grabbed a cup of coffee from a street-side vendor outside the bank, chatting about the fishing weather these days as the guy poured the cup. During a conversation about marlins and groupers, Eli's fiancée arrived, stepping out of a taxicab just as Eli left the bank fifteen minutes after he'd gone in. Eli walked over to Isla and wrapped her in an embrace that became a kiss. Then he squeezed her ass, smacked it, and tugged her close.

He draped an arm possessively around her and walked down the street.

A few blocks later they darted into a local realtor's office.

CHAPTER EIGHTEEN

She met him at Happy Turtle Cove in the early evening. She'd been here already, mapping out a plan to take her group here in a few days. She'd wanted to visit the spot one more time before the tour, and she'd run into a few friends. Sandy had been here, prepping to kiteboard with Reid. She'd chatted with them for a bit, then told them she'd see them at the boat party later this week. She also spotted a big, burly guy with a snake tattoo on his arm. He was snoozing behind shades on a beach towel. The Caymans wasn't a big place, so she'd figured he was her stepdad's club manager and she'd meet him soon enough, since she hadn't when she'd visited the club.

But everyone else fell from her mind as Jake walked toward her.

Time for several deep breaths. She tried to calm her rapidly beating heart. Her tap-dancing nerves. Her flip-flopping belly. But hormones fueled her still, those raging beasts that seemed to cannibalize every brain cell when he was near. Because . . . those broad shoulders. That sexy grin. Those green eyes. That hair. Oh Lord, that hair. How would it feel to slide her fingers through it as he moved over her? How would it feel to have him deep inside her? How would she like to rip off that blue T-shirt, and unzip his cargo shorts, and wrap her hands around him?

A ribbon of heat raced through her bloodstream, answering her. *Amazing. Fucking amazing.*

"Hey," he said, then flashed a lopsided grin that made her want to kiss him again, though she knew that would lead to nothing but trouble for her heart.

"Hi," she said, and wished she had pockets on this sundress so she could have something to do with her hands that were too eager. She laced her fingers together so she wouldn't grab the man in a wildly inappropriate embrace.

"How was your day?" he asked, and she detected a note of nerves in his voice.

"Fine. You?"

"Good. Should we get you to dinner at Eli's?" he asked quickly, gesturing to his car on the other side of the sand dunes. There was a strange awkwardness in his tone.

"Absolutely," she said with a squeak.

He held out an arm, but not for her. More of a gesture for her to walk. *OK, fine.* If he wasn't making contact, perhaps he regretted yesterday.

He cleared his throat.

Uh-oh.

"I was just thinking, we should go back to—"

"Yes. Absolutely. Just focus on the work," she said, quickly rearranging her attitude in an instant, slipping on the *play-it-cool* one. While her heart ached the teeniest bit, her brain knew this was wise. She just wished she'd said it first.

He nodded crisply. "Glad we agree."

"We so agree," she said through gritted teeth, and they drove to Corey's Landing in her car. He was quiet most of the drive; then he started to speak, and she was sure he was going to admit that keeping their hands off each other was *the worst idea ever*.

Even though it was completely what they needed to do.

Completely.

One hundred percent.

"Hey, Steph. I saw Eli and his fiancée heading into a realtor's office downtown today," he said as they turned into the development and he told her about his morning. "Any chance you could try to suss out what that's about tonight? In case it's pertinent to the money and the diamonds and all?"

He was clearly focused on the job. She could absolutely do the same. She was Steph Anderson, determined as ever, confident, bold, and unafraid. She swam with turtles, she kissed stingrays, she tangoed with dolphins. She could focus on the mission—finding out about the missing money.

"Of course. I can absolutely do that. In fact, I did some research on Isla today," she said, rattling off some facts, since she was not going to be one-upped in the *just-work* department. "Isla studied art history in college and she runs this gallery now, as you know. She's very passionate about collecting modern art, and she's also a generous supporter of the charitable arm of that diamond mine," Steph said crisply, sliding into her businesswoman mind-set as she parked the car at the end of the road.

"That's an unusual combo."

"Maybe she just likes the finer things in life," she mused, then took a beat and looked at him curiously, then returned her eyes to the road. "Why did we need to meet up *before* this dinner party? You're not going in. I am. Can't I just find you afterward and tell you what I learned?"

"I told you I'd wait for you in case anything comes up," he said in a cool, even tone. "But don't worry. I know how to lie low. I'll be hiding in the rosebushes, since there's no trellis."

"No. I'm serious, Jake."

He sighed. "I just wanted to be here in case anything comes up. That's all. It's good for us to do things together."

"But you followed him this morning without me. I looked up the website without you. We don't have to do everything together," she said as she pulled to a stop in the parking lot at the development. She stared at him through narrowed eyes.

He dragged a hand through his hair. "What are you saying, Steph?"

"I'm saying I think you're babysitting me because you don't trust me."

"Are we really going back there again?"

"I don't think we ever got past there."

"No, I'm pretty sure I did, and you're the one who said you didn't trust me."

"But now it turns out you don't trust me, either."

"I just want to be here for you after the dinner."

"That hardly seems necessary. But enjoy waiting for me," she said, tapping the steering wheel. "Don't steal my car."

"Steph," he said. "That's not fair. I'm not going to steal your car."

As she opened the door, she tossed him the keys. "It's fine if you do. It's a rental, and it's insured. You really don't have to wait for me."

He stretched across the seat to grab her arm, wrapping his fingers tightly around her wrist. It felt possessive, and better than it should. The little hairs on her arm stood on end. "Steph," he said softly. "You look gorgeous tonight."

Her heart thumped. She gave it a mental swat, staying strong. "Flattery will get you nowhere."

"You make it really hard to focus on just working with you. But I know that's what you want, so I'm trying to make it easy for you. And I'm trying to make this whole thing easy for you because I can't imagine how hard it is doing what you're doing, and trying to make things right for your mom. So I'll be here, waiting."

She softened a bit. Reminded herself why she was walking into her semi-estranged stepfather's home. To do something she didn't ordinarily do. Spy. Snoop. Play Nancy Drew. Her mom might act as if she was all fine with the royal screw in the divorce, but there was no way that was true. Steph had a chance to right a wrong.

Besides, she wasn't stealing. She was merely casing the joint.

She laughed to herself. Now she was using regular old lingo. Like a pro.

∽

Perfect. She was safe and sound inside the house.

Jake had no intention of waiting in the car. He had business to take care of and he didn't want her to know what it was. If she knew what he was up to, she might act nervous. Flinch when she heard a sound. Listen for every creak in the floorboards.

She needed to walk through the door without a clue.

She was wrong about one thing, though. He trusted her. But the less she knew, the greater chance that he could pull it off as she unknowingly provided his cover.

∽

"You're here!"

Her voice was like honey and whiskey, and her body had been carved by artist's hands.

Steph walked into a full-on embrace from the model-esque Isla. The woman looped her arms around her like she was her long-lost relative.

"Hi," Steph said, as if the word itself were new to her, and it sounded that way on her tongue.

Isla was tall, toned, tan, and trim. The four *T*s. Stunning, too, and that irked Steph. Perhaps because it was so cliché, and for once she wished her stepfather would stop trafficking in clichés. Like this picturesque mini mansion perched on the edge of the water. Like his taste for showy jewelry. Like his predilection for affairs. Frustration coiled inside her, a gnawing wish that he could be the Eli she knew—the father who cared, not the man who'd hurt her mom.

Isla placed her arms on Steph's, tilted her head, and beamed. "I'm so glad you're here. I have been dying to have you meet all my friends."

Steph furrowed her brow. Friends? "Where's Eli?" she asked as her eyes darted from left to right, quickly cataloging the plush beige couch in the sitting room; then the marble table in the entryway; the chandelier hanging from the ceiling, brilliant with dangling teardrop crystals; then the white tiled floor.

She cast her gaze to the marble table, faintly wishing for that crystal bowl full of diamonds, like jelly beans.

It was nowhere to be seen.

Nor was her stepfather.

The only diamond in sight adorned the throat of Isla. Brilliant, and hanging on a pendant, it had a faint blue tint to it. Just like her stone. Same size. Same cut.

Her stomach churned as another piece of evidence met her eyes. Another $10,000 diamond. She gritted her teeth as the diamond shone on the neck of the woman who *hadn't* given Eli money to start his business. The woman who *wasn't* her mother. The latest lady in a string of affairs he'd had, each one breaking the heart of the person Steph loved most.

A new determination set in to uncover the full truth, diamonds, money, and all. Whatever Eli had done with the gems, she needed to know. She needed the truth—for her mom and for herself. So she could make peace with whoever her stepdad was.

Isla winked. "He was called away tonight on business, but it's perfect that you're here. Some of my girlfriends and I are having a little get-together," she said, and dropped her hand on Steph's shoulder, ushering her inside.

Shrieking echoed across the home, and a woman cried out in joyous laughter. "Oh my God, that feels amazing on my elbow. I can't even."

Was she testing out lotion? A new massage oil?

Isla's green eyes sparkled as she dropped her voice to a naughty whisper. "Wait 'til she tries it in other places."

Steph furrowed her brow. "Like her hands?"

"Oh yes, that's a good start."

Another voice erupted in naughty laughter. "You all need to leave now. This bad boy is going to melt all my panties."

Steph cringed. From head to freaking toe. She hadn't walked into a family dinner, but a randy ladies' night in.

No trellis needed. Thank you very much. A tree branch would do just fine. This former soldier knew how to climb a tree and catwalk across the branch like a tightrope. It hung close enough for Jake to take one more step . . . raise his foot . . . reach across . . . and there.

Safe landing.

Both feet were on the stucco roof.

Lock kit in hand, he shimmied open a bathroom window in twenty seconds flat. He climbed inside and dropped softly on the floor of a palatial bathroom suite. Smelled like expensive perfume and fancy lotions and potions, as well as the kind of aftershave that men older than he wore. A faint light from the makeup mirror provided the barest illumination of fluffy towels on hooks, a waterfall shower, and double sinks.

Nice digs.

He stood in place, his ears trained on the sounds of the house. The upstairs was quiet and still. In the distance, the faint tinkling of women's laughter fell on his ears. Steph was keeping them busy.

CHAPTER NINETEEN

"You have to see all the goodies," Isla said, clasping a hand around Steph's arm and whisking her through the dining room, where a maid with a sleek black ponytail presided over little appetizers, like tuna on a criss-cross potato chip, a bowl of olives, a plate of nuts, and mushroom caviar. In the kitchen, another woman in a black-skirted uniform tidied up.

"Have you heard of Joy Delivered?" Isla asked.

Steph blushed. Of course she'd heard of Joy Delivered. What woman with her own credit card and online access hadn't heard of the premiere sex-toy company? She owned a few of those babies. The Wild One had taken the edge off some of her most tension-filled days, while the Lola and its ten varying pulses had turned her into somewhat of an addict. An orgasm junkie—that's what those toys could make a woman. Besides, Steph hadn't been with anyone since Duke, unless you counted battery-operated boyfriends.

Or yesterday with Jake.

"Yes. I'm familiar with Joy Delivered's oeuvre," she said drily as Isla led her to the living room, where a dozen or so women were shrieking, laughing, toasting, and feeling up purple, pink, blue, and all other color and style of sex toys. She drew a deep, fueling breath, reminding herself she'd been invited behind enemy lines tonight. This was her chance to learn, to observe, to soak up as much intel as possible.

"Isla, look! This one has ten speeds, and it simulates a tongue," a bleached blond with a penchant for Botox shouted to the hostess. Her forehead didn't move as she spoke. It appeared to have been ironed on.

"Oh, that sounds amazing," Isla purred in that sultry voice. "I should try that with my sweetie."

Sweetie. Eli.

Was that Steph's lunch that was coming back up? Yes, it might very well be. She squeezed her eyes shut momentarily, then opened them and plastered on a smile as the women passed the Lola toy around.

"That's one of the best models," an authoritative-sounding brunette with cat's-eye glasses pronounced. She must be the sex-toy representative. "It's made of the finest silicone and it'll last at least ten hours before you need to charge it or change batteries. Ten hours—do you know how many orgasms that equals?" she asked, like a teacher tossing out a question to the class.

Bleached Blonde waved her arm high. "Pick me, pick me."

"Madeline, tell us," the woman said.

The blonde sat up straighter and turned her index finger and thumb into an *O*, declaring, "With my ex-husband, it's zero. With my hot new boy toy, it's infinity."

The ladies cracked up, and Isla grabbed Steph's arm once more. "Isn't that so true," Isla said breathlessly. "It's the same for me. Well, Eli's no boy toy, but he's all man in the—"

"Is that champagne? I have been craving it all day," Steph said, as if she'd had nothing but the bubbly beverage on her mind. She pointed to a bottle on the sleek pewter coffee table.

"Someone get this hot young babe a champagne," Madeline shouted, pointing at Steph.

In seconds, Steph had downed the bubbly beverage and figured she'd need many more to make it through a sex-toy party that her stepfather had inadvertently invited her to. Or perhaps it was intentional. The mere thought of that made her pour a second glass.

⁓

Easy as pie.

Padding quietly down the carpeted hall, as noiseless as a cat, Jake passed a guest bedroom, then reached the office. Holding his breath, he gripped the doorknob and turned it quietly. Every muscle in his body was poised. To move, to run, to respond. Logic told him that Eli wouldn't be in this room, but you never know.

Gently, he opened the door and peered beyond it. The moonlight streaked through the window, casting faint glows across the desk, the floor, and the shelves.

Photos of Eli's fiancée and his kids lined his desk. An image of Steph kissing a stingray caught Jake's attention. The sun shone on her face, and the water sparkled like diamonds behind her. Her smile could launch a thousand ships. Her happiness radiated from the frame, and his heart beat faster.

He smacked his chest to shut it up.

The safe had to be in here. He began his search.

⁓

The bleached blonde named Madeline patted the seat next to her. "You're Eli's girl, right?"

"Stepdaughter," Steph corrected as she took the seat.

The dark-haired maid swooped in and deposited a new tray full of appetizers on the low table. Immediately, Isla's hand shot out for the olives, with fingers like a pelican's beak, grasping one. She popped it into her mouth and rolled her eyes in delight.

"Tell us everything," Madeline said. "He talks about you all the time."

A chorus of women's voices echoed Madeline.

"He does?" Steph asked as happiness coursed through her.

Isla nodded. "He was so excited to see you earlier this week at Tristan's."

Steph parted her lips, tempted to ask why he'd invited her tonight but didn't show. Instead, she focused on her mission. "I was so happy to see him, too. It sounds like you're both having the time of your lives here in the Islands," she said, grateful that the light-headedness from the champagne made her sound truly thrilled.

Isla placed her hand on her heart. "Oh, we are. We truly are. Life is lovely in the Caymans."

Steph sighed happily, imitating Isla. "I can only imagine. You have the club, and he told me about all your charitable work, and of course the property you're investing in, too," she said, the words tumbling forth with ease as she went fishing for info. The rest of the women oohed and aahed as they stroked pearl-filled rabbits and dual-action toys.

Isla's eyes lit up and she crossed her fingers. "I'm hoping and praying the deal goes through. Madeline is my realtor, so I have high hopes. And when it does, I should be able to expand my gallery and showcase even more world-class art."

"Oh, won't that just be divine!" Steph declared, the bubbles buoying her as she mentally patted herself on the back for reeling in that bit of intel about their real-estate ventures. Jake would be impressed. Sexy, smart, hands-off Jake, who was waiting patiently in her Jeep.

"Yes. I do hope so. I've sold several paintings recently from an artist named Lynx who has such a brilliant concept of what the world can be."

"How so?" Steph asked, eyes pinned on Isla.

"He believes in simplicity. That the world and its challenges can be reduced to geometric shapes. Eli and I so agree with him. He's on a retreat in California to meditate on his newest series."

Ah, so that explained the art in the club. Steph reached for her glass, downing the rest of it. "That must be where Eli is tonight. At the gallery," Steph said, casting the bait in the water once more.

Isla waved a hand dismissively. "Oh, he got called away into the club. Had to check on a security issue there. You can never be too careful, you know."

Steph's ears pricked. Isla was like a blessed font of information. "Of course. One must always be safe. Can't skimp on security."

Isla patted Steph on the knee. "He'll be back. He won't stay away for long, knowing I'm doing some shopping tonight for new friends," Isla said, waggling her well-groomed eyebrows at the array of vibrators.

She coughed. Lunch was definitely making a return trip. "Excuse me for a minute. I need the ladies' room."

"Just head down the hall," Isla said, gesturing grandly, the ring on her right hand sparkling as she pointed.

Steph wandered past the kitchen, glancing behind her to make sure the coast was clear, then into the long hallway. Like a true Nancy Drew, she hunted around, scanning for any hidden doorways, secret passageways, or for art that might house a safe. The walls were lined with framed images of shapes—it was an homage to basic geometry with paintings of squares, circles, and trapezoids, similar to the club. But they were miniature—a few inches wide by a few inches high, too small to hide a safe. Crap. She really wanted to find a possible location for diamonds.

Now, let's see. If she were a safe, where would she be? She tapped her fingers against her chin as she peered around. Taking quick steps, she hurried down the hall when someone opened a door.

The safe was small, hidden on a bookshelf behind a series of coffee-table photograph books of remote island locations. It took all of two minutes and twelve seconds to crack. Jake held his breath as he gingerly opened the small metal door. His heart beat loudly against his rib cage and that dangerous thing known as hope dared to surface inside him. What a thrill that would be to find a velvet pouch full of the money—in the form of diamonds—that Eli stole from Bob in Middle America.

He patted around the safe and found a passport.

OK, fine. Safes were excellent places to store important identification. He stuck his hand in farther, and holy smokes. That was what Eli had in his safe?

⌒୭

Her pulse spiked as she bumped into another woman in the hall. The brunette sex-toy mistress.

"Oh hi, Steph," the woman said. "I was just getting some more goodies from my car. I didn't expect them to sell so quickly. But I can't complain."

"Oh well, who doesn't need to buy a dildo?" Steph joked as her cheeks burned bright red.

"I do hope you'll get something. And as the daughter of the house I'll happily give you a discount."

Steph shook her head. "Stepdaughter. And I'm all good. Really. Bought a few dozen butterflies last week at a clearance sale, so I'm good to go," she said, then pointed to the bathroom door. "I'm just going to pop into the restroom."

Once inside, she did her best to take a while, washing her hands and applying some hand lotion when she was through. That should buy her some time to have the hallway to herself. But when she left, the woman was there, waiting to see her back to the party.

"Here," the woman said, reaching into the box and taking out a black velvet bag. "Just take it. It's on me."

Steph shook her head. "Oh no. I can't."

"Please. It would make me happy to give you a gift."

Steph parted her lips to protest, but the woman was insistent, staring intently at her over her glasses. "Thank you."

"The pleasure is all mine. By the way, I'm Monica. I hope you enjoy your new gift. Let's go back to the party," she said, and nudged Steph gently with her elbow, guiding her back into the cackling fest of buzzed, horny women. So much for safe hunting. Monica had safe-blocked her.

Madeline gestured excitedly as they returned to the toy fest. "Did you get it? The piece de resistance?"

"I did," Monica said in a sex-kitten voice. She set down the big box, dipped her hand inside, and took out a small black box that looked distinctly like the one Eli had given Steph with the diamond in it. Her spine straightened and adrenaline tripped through her blood. Monica popped open the top, and the women gasped.

"Oh, it's gorgeous."

It was gorgeous. *Blinding* was another word that worked. Brilliant, too. Inside the box was a jewel, but it was bigger than the one her stepfather had given her. Brighter, even.

But something about it looked decidedly fake.

Leave no trace.

That was his mantra, and he had successfully lived up to it tonight, closing and locking the safe, rearranging the books in front of it, and shutting the office door behind him. He exited the house through the bathroom window, crouched along the roof, and climbed into the tree. Mere seconds later, he walked across the spongy grass, having covered his tracks.

OK, he didn't entirely leave no trace. He'd taken something from the safe. He *had* to show Steph.

⟝◡

Isla made grabby hands, and Monica gave her the small box. "Look. It's rhinestone-studded. Eli's going to be so surprised. He's going to love it so much."

Isla pulled the jewel out of the box.

No. Please no. Oh God. Say it isn't so.

"I can't wait to give this to him, Monica. He loves this kind of play. He's going to be so excited. We're going to use it tonight."

Steph smacked her forehead. "Oh, excuse me. I forgot I have a late-night dive. Must go."

Intel was one thing. TMI was entirely another.

CHAPTER TWENTY

She marched down the stone path, around the front of the house, and walked smack into the hardest, firmest chest she'd ever felt.

"Did you find the jelly beans?"

"No. I stumbled into a gaggle of middle-age women in bandage dresses with huge egg-shaped rings ogling dolphins, rabbits, and butt plugs. Then, I got stymied by a sex-toy mistress, who followed me to the ladies' room—"

"She didn't join you in there, did she?"

Steph swatted his arm. Jake's very strong, very muscular, very toned arm. "No! She didn't join me in the bathroom. But she waited for me. To give me a goddamn sex toy," she said, thrusting the velvet pouch at him.

Jake raised his eyebrows. "Tell me more."

She shot him a stare that could crumble steel. "Go ahead. Look inside. Feel free."

He shrugged happily and opened the drawstring. "That's what we call sneaking in through the back door."

Despite her irritation, she managed a small laugh. "For a minute there, I almost thought we had the answer to where the diamonds are. But this gem is fake."

"Somewhere out there, though, someone is making gold-plated dildos. Diamond-encrusted vibrators. Rabbits filled with real pearls," he said, shaking his head in mock wistfulness as they headed to her car. "Speaking of diamonds in the house, did you have any success?"

She cut him off, slicing her hand through the air. "No. No. No. And more no. Did you not hear me? The sex-toy mistress practically clung to me, and then I was very nearly subjected to a discussion of Eli's predilections." She dragged a hand through her hair in frustration. "I did not find the bowlful of diamonds, so we'll have to go back again, and my champagne buzz is nearly gone, so I could really use a Cherry Popsicle."

"Is that code for a ruby-encrusted—"

"No. There's a bar along the beach that serves frozen cherry margaritas and they're called Cherry Popsicles because they're made around a frozen block of cherry ice, and when you get to the end you can suck on the Popsicle in the middle of it, and if I do not get one stat, my brain will be permanently branded with images of my stepfather's fiancée holding *that thing*," she said, gesturing wildly at the black pouch.

"Fair enough. To the Cherry Popsicle purveyor we go. Do they have ice cream? I do love a good ice-cream cone."

"I'll find you ice cream, Jake."

"By the way, what's a bandage dress? Is that like a dress made out of Band Aids?"

She heaved a sigh. "No. It's a style. It's very clingy and tight, but the fabric is sturdy," she said, stopping to point to her breasts as if to show how a bandage dress would hug her curves.

He cleared his throat, and when she looked up, she saw him looking down.

At her boobs.

"I forgot. You're a boob starer. Didn't mean to tempt you, since you're trying to stay on the wagon."

He held up his hands in mock surrender. "One, you say that like it's a bad thing. Two, you have fantastic breasts. And three, do you blame me? You were waving your hands in front of them. I had no choice but to stare at them."

She tugged his arm and resumed her walk, wishing she didn't like it so much that he enjoyed the view.

Once inside the car, he smiled at her like a cat who'd caught the tastiest mouse in the universe.

"What?" She held her arms out wide. "What's the smile for? The velvet pouch? The boob stare?"

"Just wanted to say thank you."

"For what?" she asked, furrowing her brow.

His grin spread across his whole handsome face. It lit up his eyes. They twinkled with mischief. "The diamonds aren't in the house. We don't have to go back."

She cocked her head to the side. "What do you mean?"

"You did an excellent job."

"At what?" The hair on her arms stood on end.

"At getting info about the first floor of the house."

"Jake, what are you getting at? Just say it," she said. "What do you mean about the first floor?"

He shrugged happily. "I took care of the second floor."

Her eyes popped, her jaw dropped, and her brain went haywire. "What?"

"I climbed in through the second-story window and checked out his office. Want to know what he keeps in his safe?"

Equal parts surprise and curiosity ripped through her. "You were in there the whole time I was there, and you didn't tell me?"

"I wanted you to be able to act natural and not worry about my poking around upstairs and trying to break into a safe."

"You tricked me again!" she shouted, grateful they were in her car, parked at the end of the block.

"That's one way to look at it. But I like to think I was protecting you."

"From what?" She crossed her arms.

"From you inadvertently letting on that the guy you're teamed up with was sneaking around upstairs and cracking your stepdad's safe."

She shook her head and breathed out hard. She couldn't believe that's what he had been up to while she was parked in the midst of the sex-toy ladies. But yet, she couldn't deny his plan was brilliant. Nor could she deny her curiosity any longer.

"What did you find?"

He reached into his back pocket and pulled out a chocolate bar. The wrapper said it was from Ecuador. "He has a few dozen of these in his safe, along with his passport. I grabbed one from the top. Didn't want him to notice they were gone and start worrying."

She studied the chocolate, tapping the bar. "That's the chocolate he invested in that went belly-up, right?"

"Guess he likes it, and held onto a few for himself," Jake said with a shrug.

She laughed. "He always did like his sweets."

"Can't blame him on that account."

CHAPTER
TWENTY-ONE

Steph sucked on a cherry Popsicle.

Steph sucked on a cherry Popsicle.

Steph sucked on a cherry Popsicle.

Try as he might, his brain was stuck on repeat. His eyeballs were glued to the scene in front of him. Steph, licking the Popsicle. Her tongue swirling along the length of the cherry ice. He shifted on the picnic table bench, trying to adjust his shorts.

Futile effort.

It was fucking tight in there. He'd been hard since he first saw her tonight, then again when she waved her hands in front of her fantastic breasts, and now ever since she'd started licking the frozen treat.

Then she emitted a moan of culinary delight. And rolled her eyes.

Rock. Hard.

Not. Fair.

He did not know why he'd suggested they focus on just work. She was all he could focus on right now. He could barely remember why getting involved on a job was a bad idea. Couldn't possibly be a bad idea. His body thought it was a very good idea.

"Enjoying yourself?" he asked as he finished his mint chocolate chip ice cream.

"This is heavenly. You really should have one."

"Yeah, I should. But one of us needs to drive," he said, taking the final bite of his cone. "Besides, this mint chip rocks my world."

"Told you so," she said, waggling her eyebrows. "I can't believe you're not going to try a Popsicle, though. What if you had one, and then we talked about our plans for an hour, and then you could drive?"

"Nah. Can't take a chance. But by all means, continue fellating the Popsicle."

"I do believe I will." She drew the Popsicle in deep and sucked long and hard.

He scrubbed a hand over his jaw. "Killing me," he muttered.

She cocked her head to the side. Affixed a quizzical look. "How am I killing you, Jake? I thought you wanted to go back to *just work?*"

"I said that. I meant it. I also find you insanely attractive. Therefore, the conundrum."

"A conundrum indeed," she said, flicking her tongue across the ice.

A night breeze blew by, and strands of her hair danced lazily around her shoulders. He supposed he could have looked away. He could have gazed contemplatively at the crescent moon and its sickles of light spotlighting the vast waters at night. Or at the vacationers strolling by along the beach. Even at the tiki torches that flickered at the edge of the bar that sat perched on the sugary white sand.

But she was some kind of temptation, and looking away was damn impossible. He steepled his hands together and did his darnedest to focus on work. "Let's talk about chocolate bars, and real estate, and art galleries."

"My stepdad must really like those chocolate bars to keep them socked away in a safe. But it's totally his style. He had a Tupperware container full of his favorite French chocolate that he kept on a high shelf so Robert and I wouldn't take it."

"Did that stop you?"

She laughed and shook her head. "Nope. We were determined little kids. Climbed up on chairs and the counter to get the sweets. He always had good sweets."

"Should we try it? See if it's any good?"

She crinkled her nose. "What if it's the worst chocolate in the world? What if it's poisoned?"

He arched an eyebrow. "You tell me if that seems likely that your stepdad keeps a safe full of poisoned chocolate."

She gestured with her fingers for him to give her some. "Fine. I'll be the guinea pig. I'm not afraid. Give me a bite."

Not wanting to let her lab rat alone, he broke off chunks of the bar for each of them. Setting aside the Popsicle, Steph bit into hers, and Jake did the same. The chocolate was delicious.

Steph pointed to the bar. "Damn, that's good," she said as she finished it.

"No wonder he keeps a secret stash locked up."

"He was always an odd duck. Like I've said, he loves his luxuries, so to him, maybe this chocolate is his luxury."

"Maybe it is," Jake said, and he wasn't sure it was worth spending any more time wondering *why* Eli stowed his chocolate—the reason was apparent in the taste. "But at least we know what's in his safe, and what's *not* in his safe."

"And so we look elsewhere. Eliminating locations is just as important, right?" she said, and there was such a sweet earnestness in her voice that simply latched onto his heart. Like she wanted to impress him. Like she wanted to show she knew what she was doing.

That was a change.

Up until now, she'd seemed reluctant to truly hunt for the diamonds. She'd been clinging to some notion of absolution for her stepdad, but for the first time, he saw a real determination in her eyes, and heard it in her voice.

He liked it. Liked it a lot.

"Yes, absolutely. Tell me what you learned at the sex-toy party," he said, resting his palms on the wood of the table and listening to her talk. She segued into work mode quickly, too, telling him what she uncovered about the gallery expansion plans, as well as her stepfather's security concerns at the club. Then he told her what he suspected from this morning's bank recon. "My original thought was he kept the diamonds at the house and, bit by bit, batch by batch, had been converting them into money. But he must keep them elsewhere or he moves them in small batches. The next thing to do is to figure out where else they might be."

She snapped her fingers. "Penny! She used to do some work for my dad. She's supposed to be at the boat party later this week. We could talk to her. She might know something."

Damn, she was indeed changing her tune.

He smiled. "Perfect. You seem more gung-ho than you were before."

She shrugged. "I suppose it's the cherry Popsicle. Or it might be seeing the diamond on Isla's throat. Made me mad."

Anger was good. He could work with that.

"I still don't want him to go to prison, though," she said.

Jake held up his hands. "Not my job to put people behind bars. I work around the law, not for the law."

"You're not going to turn him in to the SEC or something?"

He laughed, shaking his head. "I work for clients, not government agencies. When I find the diamonds, I return them to their rightful owners. Andrew and the Eli Fund. Simple as that."

She quirked up the corner of her lips, as if she was considering all he'd said. Then she nodded. "Fair enough." She picked up her Popsicle, licked it one last time, then set the stick on the table. She placed her chin in her palms. "OK, let's play truth or dare." She waved her hand in the air. "Wait. No. Just truth."

He rolled his eyes. "You're pissed that I didn't tell you what I was planning tonight?"

She held up her thumb and forefinger to show a sliver of space. "It feels a teensy bit deceptive."

He leaned forward. "Steph, I did it because I knew we'd have a better chance of pulling it off if you didn't know."

"Do you think I'm not a good partner?" she asked, her gaze intensely serious. "Tell the truth."

He scoffed. "I think you're great."

"But yet you didn't think I could pull off being in the house and knowing you were there."

"Next time I'll tell you. Does that work for you?"

She nodded. "Good. Now, the next truth. How was it?"

"How was what?"

"Sneaking into his house?"

"Fun," he said, since that was wholly true. His job came with an adrenaline rush that he craved.

Her gaze drifted to his arm, and the scar he'd recently acquired. "Truth again. That's not from a fishing accident, is it?"

He held up his hands in surrender and laughed.

"How did it happen? Tell the truth this time. If you even can," she said, but her tone was teasing, and he sensed they'd moved beyond her annoyance over feeling tricked. Especially when she dropped her hand to his wrist and ran a finger along the scar.

He shook his head. "Knife fight in Paris. Couple of thugs who stole a Strad."

"Did it hurt?"

"At the time, yes."

"And now?" she asked, running her fingertip along the line of raised white flesh. His breath hitched.

"No," he whispered.

He blinked and did a double take when a brunette walked by. She wore cat's-eye glasses, and something about her looked familiar. Then he remembered. She was the woman who helped him at the diamond shop. Monica.

He took Steph's hand. "Truth or dare?"

She flashed him a grin. "Dare."

"I dare you to go for a walk on the beach with me."

"I thought we were trying to focus on work, not on ridiculously romantic situations that are going to make it hard for you to resist throwing yourself at me?"

He laughed, loving her sense of humor. Then he did his best job tricking himself when he said, "We can just talk shop."

He tossed some bills on the table for a tip and headed along the sand as the ocean waves gently beat against the shore in a peaceful night rhythm. "You said you appointed yourself private detective. What made you want to do that? For your mom, you said."

Steph nodded and sighed heavily. "Eli screwed around on her for years."

Jake burned. He nearly growled as he narrowed his eyes. "There's a special place in hell for people who do that."

"Maybe there is."

"Did she know about it?"

Steph shrugged. "I don't think so at first. I knew by the time I was a teenager, and I didn't want to believe it. I wanted to be wrong. He was such a good dad that I tried to deny it, telling myself maybe he just had friends who were women. Maybe they were colleagues. I didn't want to think he was cheating, that he'd hurt our family like that. I sort of hid from the truth at first, but even when it was clear what was going on, I wasn't sure if I should say something or not. Is it my place to tap my mom and say, '*Hey, your husband's screwing the assistant?*' Eventually she learned on her own, and he groveled, and she tried again. But it didn't work."

"She'd had enough of him?"

She nodded. "At that point, my brother and I were both out of the house and living on our own, so she didn't feel that obligation anymore that I think was the biggest driving factor for her in staying with him when I was younger. So they got divorced, but he's a very shrewd man and knows how to manipulate anything. He was able to get away with pretty much everything and leave her with very little."

Jake scoffed. "That's just shitty."

"Yup," she said with a nod, then ran her finger over the treasure chest necklace she wore. "We're really close. I basically adore her. She's incredibly supportive of me and my business. She made this for me. That's what she does—makes jewelry."

Gently, he brushed his thumb across the miniature treasure chest, grazing the soft skin of her chest. "It's lovely," he said. He wasn't just talking about the necklace.

She swallowed and breathed a quiet *thank you*. "And look, it's not like she's destitute from the divorce. She's not living on bread and water. But he took *everything*, and it just seems so wrong. My God, she helped him start his business with money she earned from selling jewelry at craft fairs."

"It's completely wrong. Completely unfair. Especially when she made his business and livelihood possible," he said, agreeing.

"She's very giving and very generous, and that's one of the things I love about her. That's why I came here early to try to figure out what happened with the money. Like I'm Robin Hood or something. And that's why I want to help—" Then she stopped talking. Like she'd simply sliced off the end of the sentence.

"Are you OK?" he asked gently, as his heels dug into the sand. He placed a hand on her elbow. He was unable to stop touching her.

"Why am I telling you this?" she asked, but the small smile forming on her lips gave her away. She wanted to trust him.

"Because I'm easy to talk to," he said, wiggling his eyebrows. He turned serious. "You haven't mentioned your dad. Is he gone?"

She nodded. "He died of a heart attack when I was three. Never really knew him."

He squeezed her hand. "Sorry to hear that."

"Thanks," she whispered, then sighed deeply, as if the air were refueling her. "What about you? Why do you do this?"

"This is just a job for me," he said, trying to keep his tone even.

She turned to him and knocked on his forehead.

"Knock. Knock."

He laughed. "Fine. I'll take the bait. Who's there?"

"I don't believe a word you're saying, that's who."

"Just a job," he repeated, toeing his own party line. He didn't like to give up pieces of himself. He'd been burned the last time he let someone in.

But this woman wasn't going to let him get away with that.

She stopped in her tracks and parked her hands on his shoulders. "Nothing is just a job," she said, tipping her forehead to the inky black of the sea at night, starlight dancing across the water. "Take what I do. I do adventure tours because I love it. But also because the water is where I've always felt most at home, especially after my dad died. It's this very special place to me. The ocean made me feel peaceful again, and it felt like a part of me. The part that made me whole. So what's your story, Jake Harlowe? It's only fair. We partnered up, and you know my motivation. I want to know what your story is. All I really know about you is that you have two sisters and you're kind of a recovery specialist."

He heaved a sigh and pointed to the sand. *Walk and talk.* Here it went. Serve up a piece of yourself. This wasn't something he did terribly often. He didn't like to revisit the shittiest days of his life. But she'd been honest, and he owed it to her to do the same.

"I have a little brother, too. There are four of us. And I do what I do because I'm good at it. Because it pays the bills. Because my older sister and I are responsible for my younger sister and younger brother."

"Ah," she said with a nod, an understanding one as she quickly processed what this meant. "When did your parents die?"

"They were killed by a drunk driver when I was in high school."

She cringed. "Oh no. I'm so sorry." She reached for his arm again, wrapping her hand around it as they walked through the sand.

"And the fucker got away with it," Jake added through gritted teeth. A bout of long-simmering tension curled through him, winding in his veins, twisting through his blood as memories flashed before him.

The cops at the door.

The knock.

The solemn look on their faces as they took off their blue caps, came inside, and told them the news. Died on impact. The car had skidded off the road and wrapped itself around a tree.

"I was seventeen, Kate was eighteen, and the younger ones were only seven and eight."

"Wow. I can't even imagine. That's so sad. Did they find the guy?"

He breathed in sharply. "Yes, but nothing happened."

Those words—nothing happened—contained all his anger, all his frustration, and all his reasons.

"What do you mean?"

"He was some twenty-three-year-old trust-fund baby, smashed out of his mind, and he lawyered up and got away with it. I think, if memory serves," Jake said, sarcasm dripping from his tone, "he did have to put in fifty hours of community service. Reshelving books at the library. I'm sure that taught him a big lesson."

Steph huffed. "Amazing how just hiring a lawyer and fighting like an asshole can enable you to get away with stuff." She squeezed his arm. "And that's why you do what you do? Because you don't like it when the bad guys get away with it," she said, and she got it. Not like it was hard to connect the dots, but it was a relief not to have to.

"I guess I've found my own way to try to see justice done."

"You're Batman," she pronounced, and that made him laugh. The serious moment started to fade away, like grains of sand pulled out to sea. "So that makes us Batman and Robin Hood, then?"

"Seems like it. Except I don't have that weird nipple armor."

She stopped walking, darted out her hand, and splayed it around the fabric of his shirt. She pretended to assess his nipple armor, or lack thereof. "Confirmed. The subject does not have nipple armor. However, he does have insanely hard pecs, and quite possibly the firmest chest we've ever felt."

He chuckled deeply as he backed up, leaning against a lifeguard stand, unoccupied at this late hour. The bar wasn't far away, but he felt like they were in their own corner of the night. He couldn't deny there was something nice about the moment shifting so seamlessly from heavy to light. That the harder conversation was had, and they weren't going to linger or wallow in it. They were speeding toward the path of innuendo again and that had its own risks.

CHAPTER
TWENTY-TWO

He clasped his hand over hers, tugging her closer.

"This whole *just-work* thing is working out really well, isn't it," he said in a low voice as he held her hand against his body. He craved her touch. Hell, right now, a part of him seemed to need it. Not just that insistent organ in his pants knocking on his fly. But his heart. *That* organ. Because he liked this woman. Liked her humor. Liked her heart. He still didn't want to get involved on a job . . . but he knew one thing for sure—he wanted her.

Badly.

Despite all the reasons he was supposed to stay away from complications, he was having a hell of a time walking away. Maybe it was foolish, maybe it was risky, but this second, being with her felt only right.

"Incredibly well," she whispered, running her thumb in a circle across his chest.

"Steph," he said in a warning.

"Jake," she said, like she was pushing back. "I thought we agreed . . ."

"We did." He guided her hand across his chest and down to his stomach.

She inhaled sharply as she traced his stomach, her touch like a torch, setting his nerves aflame. He tried so damn hard to be practical, to be focused, to refuse to give in. He had a job. He had responsibilities. But he didn't know if he'd last any longer holding out. "You have sand here," he said, pointing to her ear. His voice came out like dust.

She ran her finger over it. But missed.

"No. Right there," he said, reaching for her ear and brushing off the grains, and then catching a faint whiff of that coconut smell again. Drove him wild. He let his fingers drift into her hair. Looped them farther, cupping the back of her head. "What is it about you that I can't resist? Your kisses are my kryptonite."

He wrapped his hands in her hair, grasping the back of her skull as he kissed her on the beach by the lifeguard stand. Her lips were delicious, all cherry sweet from the Popsicle. As he deepened the kiss, she murmured against his lips, kissing back with all she had. It was a kiss you'd write home about or watch on a movie screen. He couldn't even pinpoint what made it so damn good. He couldn't deconstruct the kiss and say it was the shape of her lips, or the softness of her tongue, or the depth of the kissing.

It was something else entirely.

Something unknown. Something that drove him on. She kissed with such passion, such vulnerability, as if his kisses were the only ones she wanted, the only ones that would ever make her feel this way. She held nothing back as she melted into his arms and pressed her body to his in a full-body kiss—lips, tongue, hands, hips. Every part of her aligned with every part of him.

Even though they were fully clothed on the beach, she started rubbing against him, her crotch grinding into his erection. His body thrummed with lust. Whatever reasons he'd had not to touch her again seemed woefully unimportant compared to the rush of heat in his veins from her closeness.

"You taste so good," he whispered hotly as he broke the kiss.

She flashed him the sexiest grin. "So do you." She ran her fingers along his jawline, tracing his stubble and brushing her thumb across his face. Even that small touch turned him on fiercely. This was risky, but yet, his brain was urging him to roll the dice.

Or maybe it was his dick calling the shots.

He cupped her ass and tugged her closer, and soon, she was practically riding him vertically by the lifeguard stand. She moaned into his mouth, and his erection knocked against his shorts. He broke the kiss, grabbed her hand, and climbed up the lifeguard stand.

"Jake," she whispered with a naughty grin.

"What? The view's better up here. I can see the water perfectly," he said as he sat down on the weatherworn white wood and held her hand as she reached the last rung. "Climb on top."

They were far enough away from the bar that they weren't making a spectacle of themselves, and the dark of the night shielded them the rest of the way. He tugged her on top of him, so she straddled him, her knees pressing into the wood.

"Ride me," he said in a low voice.

She arched an eyebrow, asking an unspoken question.

No, he didn't expect her to fuck him like this, though the image sent blood to all the right places. But he wanted her close, wanted to answer the call he felt in her body. Her need. Her desires.

"Like this?"

"Yes."

Like high school. Like college. Like dry humping. Which could be pretty fucking awesome when you wanted a woman with this kind of intensity. She lifted her skirt and pressed against his hard-on through his shorts.

He wrapped his hands around her rear and squeezed, then pulled her closer, guiding her moves. She parted her lips, a sexy sigh escaping as she rocked against him, the full length of his erection against her wet panties. She swiveled her hips and jammed down hard on him.

"I've been picturing this," he said as she rocked back and forth against his hard-on.

"Just like this? Clothes on?"

"On. Off. Doesn't matter. Ideally off. But I'll take this," he said, groaning as she picked up speed. "You look so fucking hot on top of me and you feel incredible." He could only imagine how fantastic she'd feel when he was buried deep inside her, her wetness gripping his dick. Desire crashed wildly through his body as she moved faster, building friction, seeking release. "I bet you'd look crazy hot under me with your legs spread, and you begging me to slide into you and fuck you 'til you come hard."

Her pretty green eyes widened, and for a moment he wondered if he'd gone too far. If his dirty words and filthy thoughts were too much for her. But she didn't answer him with words. Instead, she answered by rocking her pelvis faster on him. She dropped her face to his neck and layered soft little kisses there.

Kisses that drove him wild.

She reached his ear. "Two," she whispered, and he knew what she meant.

"Go for it."

"I want to come like this," she whispered like it was a naughty confession.

"Do it," he said, like a command. "So no one hears you but me."

No way was she going to do this. She could not, would not, dry hump him to orgasm outside on a beach. But she was doing it anyway, riding him with her clothes on, craving more of his sweet dirty talk. "Tell me how much you want me to come," she said, her voice sounding like it belonged to someone else as she talked to him in ways she'd never spoken to a lover before.

"So. Fucking. Much," he said, his strong arms looped around her, his hard length pressing between her legs, his sexy growl in her ear. "I love the way you look when you lose control. How your lips part," he said, narrating her own path to orgasm as her lips fell open. "How your breathing turns fast," he continued, and her breaths came quickly. "How you rock against me wildly, your hips going crazy."

"Oh God," she said, gasping as she chased her own orgasm, racing after it, like a comet, grabbing its tail and holding on for dear life as it flew. She started to shout his name, and in a second his palm was on her mouth, so she screamed into the silence of his hand as she came undone on him in a wild frenzy of silence and heat.

She would not be deterred tonight. As soon as they reached Happy Turtle where his car was parked, she dropped her hand to his shorts, cupping his erection.

"I have to tell you something," she began, stroking him through his clothes.

He moaned. "Is this truth or dare?"

"Truth. And it's this. That ratio just got compressed."

"Is that so?" he asked, arching an eyebrow.

"That is so. Because tonight we're going to be two-to-one." She moved in close and whispered in his ear. "I want my turn. I want you."

"Steph," he said in a low warning.

"Jake. Resistance is futile."

"Does it feel like I'm resisting?"

"No. It feels like you're dying for me to wrap my lips around you," she said, unzipping his shorts in a flash.

He grabbed her hand, stopping her. "In the car?"

"In the car?" she repeated, imitating his deep voice. "Yes, like you did to me yesterday. Think of it as my evening the score."

"But I've given you two orgasms," he said playfully, but then he stopped talking when she sneaked her hand into his boxer briefs. She bit her lip as she felt him for the first time. Holy hard-on. Holy size. Jake was packing some serious inches. She'd sensed it from rubbing up against the full length of him, but now with her bare hands wrapped around him, she had the confirmation. She ran her hand up and down him, hot and heavy to the touch. Fireworks ignited in her, setting off a new round of sparks all over her body just from this—from the moment of contact.

"Lower your seat," she said, and he obliged, dropping the driver's seat to a fully reclined position.

"Take your shorts off," she continued, thrilled to give him orders.

With his big hands, he pushed his shorts down to his knees, and she licked her lips as she admired the view for the first time. It was fantastic.

"Anything else you need me to do?" he asked wryly.

She shook her head, wrapped her hand tightly around the base, and met his eyes. "No. Just enjoy yourself," she said, and lowered her mouth to his hard-on, flicking her tongue against the head.

He drew a sharp breath, and a sexy moan landed on her ears. That was her cue to continue, so she wrapped her lips around him, so damn eager to give back at last. She drew more of him into her mouth, savoring the moans and groans he made. He was not a quiet man, and that was music to her ears.

"Ah, just like that, and use your hand, too," he murmured as he threaded his fingers into her hair.

She followed his directions, loving that he gave them, because she wanted this to be as good for him as he'd been to her.

"Harder, Steph. Do it harder," he said, clasping his hand around her skull and moving her mouth up and down. "Take me deeper," he said in a throaty rumble, then whispered, all hot and husky, *"please."*

Her mouth was divine. She was an angel of mercy, and the friction was heavenly. His fingers curled around her skull, her golden blonde hair spilling over his hand as he guided her. Red-hot flames sparked in his bloodstream, and pleasure crackled through his bones as she sucked him deep. Her lips tightened around his shaft, and her tongue worked miracles, flicking and licking as she took him to the back of her throat.

"Fuck, your lips look so fucking good on me," he said on a groan. She raised her eyebrows sexily.

With one hand, he let go of his grip to sweep her hair to the side, giving him the perfect view. The sight of her mouth stretched wide, her cherry-red lips tight around his dick sent heat tearing through his body. Electricity sparked in his bones as he filled her warm mouth. Her hand wrapped tighter, and the tension in him coiled, rising higher and faster.

He could barely take it anymore. The sight of her mouth sucking him like that, her hand fisting the base, and her hair a wild tumble, drove him crazy. With barely a thread of control left, he thrust up into her, fucking her mouth.

He was going to come any second.

Words failed him. He was reduced to moans uttered in a ragged voice, desperate for release.

His own climax crashed into him, and he gripped her hair and groaned her name as he came hard.

He shuddered from the aftershocks. Seconds later, he pulled her off him and planted a kiss on her lips. "You rock my world," he said to her, and trust or no trust, it was all too true.

"Like mint chip ice cream?" she asked.

"Better."

CHAPTER
TWENTY-THREE

As she treaded azure blue waters, Steph splashed Jake. He stood on the edge of the boat in his swim shorts, the early evening sun glinting off his light-brown hair.

"C'mon. I don't bite," she said, then swam closer and pretended to grab his ankles, as if she were going to topple him into the ocean. The idea appealed to her. He seemed the type who might enjoy a good water toppling.

"I don't mind biting."

"You're not afraid of the water, are you?" she asked, egging him on.

"You crack me up, funny girl. Now prepare to be dunked."

"No way will you catch me," she said, pushing off the shell of the boat with her feet and skimming along the shallow water. They were early for the boat party. *Intentionally.* They'd arrived in the hopes of catching Penny before she was swept into the crowd. The boat, which belonged to Devon, was moored at the end of the dock.

Jake jackknifed into the water, stirring up small waves and sand below her. Then he chased her. She darted and weaved as fast as she could, but soon enough he stretched one long arm and hooked her ankle. Underwater, she laughed. She popped her head up, and so did he.

"Say it."

"Say what?" she said, splashing water at him.

"Say I caught the mermaid," he said with a smirk that made her grab his waist and attempt to tickle him underwater. He was impervious, though, and instead he clasped his hands over hers and tugged her in close. "Don't drive me wild in the water," he said, low and growly, like a command.

"I'll do my best, but you're the one who caught the mermaid," she whispered, loving the way his fingers gripped her waist, and his voice was just for her.

"I did catch her. I want her all to myself," he said, and she was sure they were talking in more than mere innuendo. That the undercurrent to this conversation echoed back to last night in his car, to the lifeguard stand, to the parking garage, to the kiss at Happy Turtle, and all the way back to the first night at the Pink Pelican. Dangerous though this was, she wanted the man. He'd felt like an opponent, or even a frenemy, most of the time, but something had shifted after last night. That talk on the beach had brought them closer. They'd both let down their guards, which was scary as hell. He was still after Eli, and she should probably swim away from him.

But she didn't do that. Her heart was bending toward him.

"I like when you have me," she whispered, the water making her daring, giving her some kind of liquid courage.

They swam for a few more minutes and then climbed back up on the boat. "I can see why you love it here," he said, handing her a towel. "This place suits you. It's beautiful, and peaceful, but also adventurous . . . like you." And her heart raced from the sweet compliment.

OK, she was definitely going to say something. Go out on that limb. Suggest the island tryst, when her name sounded like a trumpet, reverberating through the air.

"Steph!"

She spun around, and excitement whipped through her as she clambered out of the boat and onto the dock. A woman with bright pink hair and tattooed arms rode a mint-green beach cruiser along the wooden dock in her direction. A golden retriever frolicked by her side. The ultimate island girl and her dog had resurfaced.

Steph ran down the dock and Penny stopped pedaling, letting the bike fall to the dock. Penny raced the rest of the way to Steph, then hugged her with every fiber of her being.

"You're all I thought about under the stars," Penny said brightly, the dog bounding up by her side.

Steph laughed. "Girl, we need to do something about the fact that you're thinking about me while camping."

"I know, but I couldn't wait to see you. I made s'mores in honor of you. With my main man, Chase."

Steph wiggled an eyebrow. "I see no one has replaced the golden retriever."

"And no one ever will. Speaking of main men, what have we got here?" she asked, tipping her forehead behind Steph. Penny's gaze landed briefly on Jake, who walked toward them.

"That's my friend Jake," Steph said, pointing at him with her thumb, trying to keep it casual. "Met him snorkeling."

As Jake arrived next to them, Penny eyed him up and down. "Hello there. You're mighty handsome," Penny declared.

"And your hair is a lovely shade of pink," Jake said with a smile.

Jealousy flared in Steph. Out of nowhere. "What are you up to these days?" Steph asked, changing the subject. "I heard you worked for Eli and helped with his club, but Marie said you're using that green thumb of yours now at a flower shop."

"I did a little bit for Sapphire, but I helped out at the gallery, too. That place was crazy busy when I was there."

"They're expanding it now," Steph said nonchalantly.

"Probably because they need room for all their precious gems."

"What?" Steph's head bounced and *boinged* like a cartoon character. On coiled springs. Eyes popping out of their sockets.

Penny waved a hand in the air and emitted a *pshaw*. Like this was no big deal. Like they were talking about the weather. "He was always moving diamonds in and out of that gallery. Said he didn't want to leave them at home." She adopted Eli's over-the-top tone. *"The gallery is the safest spot for them."*

Penny laughed, and Steph worked on picking up her jaw from the wooden dock. Rearranging her features. Affecting a laugh. This was the easiest fact-finding mission ever. She didn't even have to ask. Penny had simply offered the delicious intel.

"Like in a safe? Behind the art or something? Like they do in the movies?"

Penny shrugged. "Hell if I know. I just overheard them talking. But let me tell you. He spent a lot of time checking out the frames of the art in the office at the gallery." She tipped her forehead to the boat. "Let's get the party started."

As the pink-haired woman walked ahead, Steph turned to Jake and pumped a fist in victory.

Four hours later, the sun had fallen, the moon had risen, and more than a half dozen women had flirted with Jake on the boat. As if he were the only man around. Sure, he was the most handsome, but Steph couldn't act like he belonged to her, because, well, he didn't.

She hung by the edge of the boat, bobbing in the water by the marina. Watching the inky black sea at night, she spent the party chatting with Sandy, Penny, and Reid, and sometimes Jake. With his eight o'clock shadow, ripped arms, and charming smile, he was a magnet. Women flocked to him.

Steph didn't like it. Didn't like it one bit. She pursed her lips and gritted her teeth.

By the time 10:00 p.m. rolled around, she'd had enough. She said good-bye to her friends; tapped Jake on the shoulder, since he was in the midst of a long chat with Reid; and told him she was taking off. Whatever sweetness she'd felt in the water earlier had fizzled. She was foolish to have entertained thoughts of trysts, and trust, and letting the man gunning for Eli into her heart.

He shot her a quizzical look, beer bottle in hand.

"I'm tired," she muttered, and headed onto the dock.

Seconds later, he caught up with her. "Hey. You OK?"

She shrugged.

"That's a no," he said.

"Maybe it's a yes," she said, offhand.

"You seem annoyed." He kept pace next to her as she walked toward land.

"You're observant."

"What's wrong?"

She waved a hand dismissively. "I just need to call it a night," she said, practically race-walking. "We can come up with an art gallery plan tomorrow, right? Isn't that what's important?"

"Sure. Of course."

Her frustration peaked over how easily he shifted gears. "Did you enjoy the party?" Before she could stop the words from tumbling forth, she added, "And the way all the women flirted with you?"

He stopped in his tracks and grabbed her arm. Wrapping a strong hand around her. "What are you saying?"

"Don't tell me you didn't notice. Everyone had her sights set on you."

He shook his head. "Didn't notice."

She scoffed. "I don't believe you."

He let go of her arm, held his hands out wide. "What else is new? You never believe me."

She parked her hands on her hips. "Do you blame me? You haven't been entirely forthcoming."

"All right. Let's come forth now. Ask me anything and I'll tell you."

Maybe that was too risky a suggestion. But Jake thrived on risks.

She might throw a question at him that he'd want to dodge and dart. But the fact was, he wanted her to trust him. He needed her trust.

She fixed him with a challenging stare. "Anything?"

He nodded. "Anything."

"Truth or dare?" she asked, the moonlight framing her stunning, sun-kissed face, the ocean breeze sweeping through her hair, the smell of saltwater wrapping around them.

"Truth," he said easily, reaching for his beer bottle and taking a drink as gentle waves lolled past them.

She arched an eyebrow and raised her chin. Her tough-girl stance, and it made her even sexier. Damn, she was hot when she was feisty. "Tell me the truth for real. Did you know who I was the night you met me?"

He scoffed. "I knew you were the hottest woman I'd seen in ages," he said, somehow unable to resist slipping around her question to give her a compliment.

She stared at him. "That's not the whole truth."

"Fine. I knew you were a pain in the ass."

"Gee, thanks."

"I knew you were going to drive me crazy."

"You drive me crazy, too," she countered, parking her hands on her hips.

"Sounds like we're just about even, then."

"No. We're not. Because you still haven't answered the question. Did you know who I was?"

"No," he said, setting his beer on the railing. He stepped closer to her and grasped her bare arms. Her skin was soft and warm. "I've told you a million times. No. No. And more no. And I could ask you the same damn thing, too. I could ask if you knew who I was. But I'm not asking. Because it doesn't matter right now. It doesn't matter anymore." He let go of her arms and gestured from him to her. "This? This isn't about who knew what when. It's about the fact that I can't get you out of my head." He tapped his skull. "It's about the fact that I'm not supposed to get involved on a job. It's about the fact that even if I weren't about to break that rule in spectacular fashion, I should absolutely not break it with you, of all people."

She pressed her teeth into her lower lip, and the tiniest sliver of a smile appeared on her gorgeous face. Oh hell, he was going to have a field day kissing that smile away all night long, and feeling her melt in his arms when he stripped her down to nothing. Because he was done pretending. Done holding back. Done doing anything but giving in to this electric chemistry that had the two of them in its clutches. Staying away from her was too damn hard.

"But you're going to? In spectacular fashion?" she asked, her tone soft and inviting now.

"No more questions, Steph. Your turn is up. It's mine now. So, what'll it be? Truth or dare?"

She licked her lips and raised an eyebrow. "Dare."

Smart woman. She was smarter than he was. Or maybe she just wanted the same thing—a dare to match the truth.

"I dare you to kiss me right now," he said with a grin, knowing she wasn't going to back down, because this woman backed down from absolutely nothing.

She inched closer.

He raised a hand in a stop sign. "I need to give you fair warning. This time, I'm not going to stop at just kissing you. I'm not going to stop at the backseat of the car. I'm not going to stop until I am buried deep inside you, and you're coming undone screaming my name."

Her eyes glinted. "You'd better not stop."

He was about to break a cardinal rule. He could blame it on days of island sunshine. Hell, he could claim the last few weeks of gray skies before he came here were at fault. Even chocolate could be the cause.

But as he roped his fingers in her hair and pressed his lips to hers, there was no blaming anything but the good old-fashioned fact that he was a man who wanted a woman.

CHAPTER
TWENTY-FOUR

Up the stairs. Down the hall. At the door to her room.

His lips were on her neck, making her shiver. His hands were in her hair, turning her on wildly. He couldn't stop touching her, and she wanted his hands everywhere. Loved how he was relentless in his quest to be as close to her as possible. Her whole body vibrated with desire.

As she reached into her purse for the card key, Jake scorched a trail of kisses along the back of her neck that made her knees go weak. She grasped the doorframe so she wouldn't stumble.

"You keep doing that right now, I may not even be able to get the door open," she said, her voice like a feather, her hand slipping as she tried to slide the key through the lock.

"Let me help," he said, taking the key and sliding it through.

"Showing off your lock-picking skills?"

"No. Showing off how much I want to get inside this room and have you," he said, his tone rough and commanding. He pushed open the door.

The card fell somewhere on the floor. Who knew? Who cared? She was alone in her room with him. The air-conditioning whirred faintly, and the moon glowed through the glass door of the balcony. He backed her up against the wall.

"Can't wait," he said, as if she needed an excuse for why they couldn't even make it to the bed.

He planted a searing kiss on her mouth that sent the temperature in her even higher. He broke the kiss and traveled down her body, along her neck, past her breasts and her belly. He was close. So close to where she wanted him, and she ached. Simply ached.

"Beautiful," he murmured as he kneeled on the floor, pushed up her skirt, and reached for the waistband of her pink cotton panties. Her breath turned erratic as a pulse beat between her legs. In one quick move he pulled her panties to her ankles. She barely stepped out of them before he had molded his hands to the inside of her thighs and kissed her there.

Right there.

Where she wanted him. Where she craved him.

Oh God, it felt so damn good. She cried out from the instantaneous crash of pleasure into every corner of her body. Closing her eyes, she gave in to the wild sensations racing through her. He kissed her wetness, flicking his tongue across her most sensitive spot.

Her hands shot into his hair, so soft and thick between her fingers. Quickly, they set a rhythm. She rocked against his mouth, her fingers tightening in his hair, as he licked and kissed and savored. He thrust his tongue inside her and she gasped, racing toward the edge of bliss. Seeing it, chasing it, seeking it out.

Close. So damn close.

"That's right. This is your first," he said, his deep, raspy voice thrilling her as he briefly broke contact then returned to her.

She rocked into his face, and he moaned as he consumed her. His own sounds were some of the sexiest she'd ever heard, the soundtrack of his own desire for her.

He groaned as he licked.

That was all she needed.

She shattered. Riding his face. Standing up against the wall. Him on his knees. A chorus of *oh Gods* echoing in the night, like aftershocks as pleasure rippled through her body.

He rose, cupped the back of her head, and arched a playful eyebrow. "Let's make it a double now."

She breathed out hard, still riding the waves of a powerful orgasm. "What will you do for your encore?"

The answer came as he unzipped his shorts and rolled on a condom.

Thank Christ.

He couldn't hold out any longer. Couldn't wait. Couldn't deny this.

He'd wanted her since he first laid eyes on her, and he was finally, finally, finally going to have her. She'd been under his skin all week long, and every encounter had amped up his want. Now, that desire ran deeper, beyond the physical. He liked her so much more than he should, more than he had room for in his life. But he ignored all the risks, because this moment was one he wanted to savor in his body.

Every second of it.

He rubbed his erection against her slick heat, his breath hissing at that first delirious contact. "You feel amazing," he said, then slid into her.

Better than he'd imagined. Hotter, tighter, and more intense than in his fantasies. They fit perfectly.

She gasped, her lips falling open. She looked so deliciously sexy like that, so vulnerable, too. That's what was undoing him. How much he wanted *all* of her.

"So do you," she said, that sweetness in her that hooked him coming through even now, even as he took her hard against the wall.

"I've wanted to be inside you since that first night," he said as he filled her, taking a beat to linger in the sheer pleasure of being inside her. "I've wanted to feel you gripping me." He pulled back, then thrust into her again, her eyes going hazy with lust.

She moaned his name. "What else did you want?" she asked, and her question sent the lust in him on a high-speed chase through his bones from the way she craved his dirty words.

"To feel how wet you get when I make you come again."

"I want to know what that's like, too," she whispered. "I've never known. Make me feel that way."

Oh hell, she was going to experience not just multiple orgasms, but exponential pleasure. He fully planned to deliver, and he had every intention of making her cry out in ecstasy again. He reached for her thigh, hooking her leg onto his hip. He went deeper like that, electricity surging in his veins as he drove into her.

Her nails dug into his shoulders, grasping him harder. He dropped a hand between her legs, sliding a finger against her. With that touch, her pants turned fevered, her moans frenzied, as she called out that she was coming again. Crying out his name in his ear.

Bliss. Fucking bliss.

"I love making you come," he murmured as he pressed a soft kiss to her cheek, slowing his thrusts as she came down from her high.

"It's so easy with you. Coming is so easy with you," she said breathlessly.

Masculine pride suffused him from the compliment, but also from the way she responded to his touch. Nothing was better than this kind of connection, this sort of undeniable chemistry. Unless it was one more orgasm for the woman he craved. He lifted both her legs, wrapped them around his back, and crossed the few feet to her bed.

While still fucking her.

Yep. He did it. He stayed inside her because he did not want to leave. Not 'til he attempted to send her up and over another peak. He lowered her to the bed, picking up the pace, thrusting into her.

"Wrap your legs tight around me," he told her, and she hooked her ankles over his ass as he moved inside her. He took her like that, as deep as he could, hoping to hit that magic spot inside her that could send her over the edge again.

Because hell, he was nearly there himself. If he was going to have any success at this hat trick, it needed to be now. Right the fuck now. Not later.

"Fuck. I can't hold back," he muttered, and the base of his spine ignited, his muscles tensing, as lust stormed through him, marching across his bones, taking no prisoners.

As his climax crashed into him, he heard the most glorious sound.

Her. Crying out again. Writhing beneath him. Grabbing his hair, calling his name, coming undone. "Oh God, oh God, oh God."

He was so damn happy.

He lay next to her, hot, sweaty, panting, and sated, as they floated down from the clouds.

"Third time's a charm," she said, then kissed him, and he kissed her back. Soft, slow, lingering.

"Can I stay the night?" He didn't want to leave. Couldn't imagine being elsewhere. Her room was the only place he wanted to be.

"You'd better."

They didn't fall asleep right away. They stayed up, chatting in the afterglow of great sex. Sometimes, conversations were made easier because of the endorphins already flowing. They talked about work and some of their favorite jobs. She told him about a dive trip in the Bahamas that she'd loved, and he shared more of the Stradivarius story. When he finished, she ran her fingers once more against the scar on his forearm and whispered sweetly, "I like this. It's sexy. It says you're rugged."

"You like your men rugged, Steph?" he asked, brushing a hand through her soft hair.

She shrugged, snuggling closer in his arms. He liked having her like this. He pressed his nose to her hair, inhaling her.

"I do," she said. "It says you can do things. My ex did nothing. But you—you work hard, and I like that."

He smiled. "I try. I like working, and I like that it enables me to take care of my family."

She sighed, a happy, contented sound that worked its way under his skin. That weaved through him, seducing him. He had to be careful or he would start feeling things for her. Dangerous things that he had no room for in his life.

But the way his heart tripped just being near her told him he was already there.

She turned to face him. "This is crazy," she said, gesturing from him to her. "And it's everything we said we shouldn't do."

He kissed her forehead. "I know."

"But yet you want to spend the night."

"I do. So much," he said softly, letting a sliver of vulnerability slip through. He didn't usually show this side of himself, but he couldn't find his resistance tonight. It was gone, and he was done searching for it. "For some reason, I can't fight this right now," he said softly, running a thumb over her chin. "You have your hooks in me."

She mimed latching on to him, and he laughed, then wrapped an arm around her. She felt so damn good in his arms. So right. She wasn't a bit like Rosalinda. She wasn't a mercenary. She wasn't conniving. Steph had so much at stake, so much to lose. Like him, she only wanted justice. She only wanted to do the right thing. He told himself this situation wasn't remotely similar to the Medici job, and that reassurance made it easier to say the next thing. He took a deep, fueling breath, then laid it out. "What do you say we stop fighting this and just give in for the rest of the time we're here?"

"We've done a pretty bad job at resisting," she said, tap-dancing her fingers across his chest. "So I'd say giving in to an island tryst sounds a hell of a lot more fun than fighting it. Besides, I like working with you, and I like the way you work on orgasms for me."

He chuckled deeply. "Excellent. Count on more. Because I am enjoying this so damn much. I'm enjoying *you* so much. More than I ever expected to," he said, then kissed her once more.

Soon, darkness cloaked them, and the peaceful, easy feeling with her lying in his arms almost made him forget why he was here.

The job. The jewels. The bounty he was hunting.

He fell asleep thinking of diamonds and her. Steph and diamonds, and soon the two were blurred together.

❧

Early the next morning after teeth were brushed and orgasms were administered, Steph and Jake parked themselves on the end of the bed and worked on the plan for the art gallery. The morning sun shone brightly through the sliding glass door of the balcony, lighting up the room and their work.

They had blueprints. They had a road map. They would be following it later today. In no time, they'd be Robin Hooding and Batmanning their way through the gallery right around lunchtime. The art on display was all frameless, which narrowed the location down to a storage room or office.

Jake's stomach rumbled. Steph raised her eyebrows. "I have a crazy idea," she said in a stage whisper.

"About how to get into the art gallery and find the diamonds?"

"No," she said, patting his flat belly. "It's about breakfast. What would you say to ordering some room service? This might not be a fancy hotel, but it has the best eggs and toast. And they actually have these little tiny jars of honey for the toast that are weirdly amazing."

"Say no more," he said, sweeping out his arm gallantly. "Eggs are my second favorite food in the world."

"After ice cream," she said with a wink.

"Or maybe after weirdly amazing honey," he joked.

A half hour later, wheels rolled by outside the room, then a knock sounded on another door. Steph popped up from the bed. "I think they got the wrong room," she said, heading to the door and peeking down the hall. Ah, there was the waiter with a tray and two plates of eggs and toast. She waved to him.

"Are those for us?" she asked.

"Oops," he said with an apologetic smile. "I went to the wrong room."

Standing outside the door, she signed the room service to her room, then thanked him. Back inside, she enjoyed a delicious breakfast on the balcony with a man who she was having an island tryst with.

He held up a cup of coffee as if in a toast. "To our island tryst."

"To being partners."

"To trusting your partner," he said, his gaze fixed on her.

"To three orgasms."

"Make it four next time." He downed some of his coffee, then leaned over and kissed her, lingering in the kiss, his lips exploring hers like it was the first time. A shiver of excitement raced through her. The kiss turned hotter after they finished breakfast, and he pulled her on top of him in the deck chair, and she rode him like that on the balcony to another fantastic climax.

A little while later, he tapped his watch. "I should go. I need to talk to Kylie and help her get some things sorted out tutoring-wise."

"I've got some things on my plate, too. I'm doing a stingray tour with Devon for two hours, but I'll see you at noon."

After a quick good-bye, Steph took a long, hot shower, replaying the night and the morning and what might come in the afternoon.

She turned off the water, toweled off, applied some sunscreen, and slipped into her royal blue bikini. As she pulled on a light-blue sundress, a sliver of light caught her attention out of the corner of her eye.

The door to the safe. It didn't look quite closed.

She walked over to it, tilting her head in curiosity. Light shone on the door's edge. Weird. She distinctly recalled locking the safe last time she checked on her diamond. Maybe she was just seeing things. Perhaps it had always looked that way.

Nerves flared through her, and her spine straightened. She reached for the door and nearly yanked her hand back when she discovered it wasn't locked.

Her heartbeat spiked as she wrapped her fingers around the small door. When she opened it and peered inside, the diamond was nowhere to be seen.

Jake and Steph's story continues in part two, *THE SAPPHIRE HEIST*.

ABOUT THE AUTHOR

 Lauren Blakely writes sexy contemporary romance novels with heat, heart, and humor. She is the author of nine *New York Times* bestsellers and seventeen *USA Today* bestsellers. Her series include Sinful Nights, Seductive Nights, No Regrets, Caught Up in Love, and Fighting Fire, as well as stand-alone romances like *21 Stolen Kisses* and *Big Rock*. She also writes for young adults under the name Daisy Whitney. Lauren believes life should be filled with family, laughter, and the kind of love that romantic songs promise. She lives in California with her husband, children, and dogs.